CLAUDIA AND THE WORLD'S CUTEST BABY

Caryn Pearson

Other books by
Ann M. Martin

Rachel Parker, Kindergarten Show-off
Eleven Kids, One Summer
Ma and Pa Dracula
Yours Turly, Shirley
Ten Kids, No Pets
Slam Book
Just a Summer Romance
Missing Since Monday
With You and Without You
Me and Katie (the Pest)
Stage Fright
Inside Out
Bummer Summer

BABY-SITTERS LITTLE SISTER series
THE BABY-SITTERS CLUB mysteries
THE BABY-SITTERS CLUB series

CLAUDIA AND THE WORLD'S CUTEST BABY

Ann M. Martin

SCHOLASTIC INC.
New York Toronto London Auckland Sydney

The author gratefully acknowledges
Peter Lerangis
for his help in
preparing this manuscript.

Cover art by Hodges Soileau

ISBN 0-590-22881-1

12 11 10 9 8 7 6 5 4 3 2 1 6 7 8 9/9 0 1/0

Printed in the U.S.A. 40

First Scholastic printing, May 1996

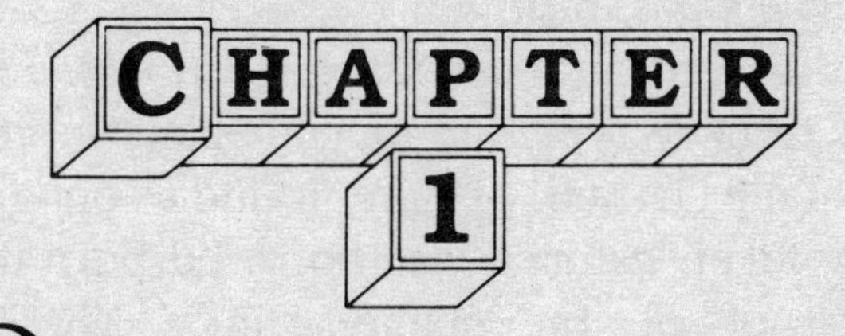

"Ohhhhh, she's so . . ."

I, Claudia Lynn Kishi, was at a loss for words. Before my eyes, an image of my aunt's baby was squeaking noisily out of my family's new fax machine. "She looks so . . ."

"Healthy," my dad offered.

"Peaceful," said my mom.

"Compressed," added my sister, Janine.

I gave her a Look. *"Compressed?"*

"Don't you think so?" she asked.

"I think she looks like her aunt," Dad remarked, beaming at Mom.

Mom looked horrified. "Thanks a lot!"

"Aw, come on," I said. "She's . . . cute."

Well, she was. I don't care what they all thought.

All right, sure, she was shriveled and gnarled and froglike. But hey, I would be, too, if I were *in utero*. (That, by the way, is a fancy term for "not born yet.") You see, my aunt was faxing us her baby's latest sonogram.

Have you ever seen a sonogram? It's a picture taken with sound waves. (I don't know how they do it. Maybe they sing through the camera.) Cool, huh?

Sort of. I mean, I can understand why you'd want to have a picture of your baby *in utero*. But let me be frank. If I ever found a sonogram of me taken before I was born, I'd burn it.

First of all, the quality stinks. My little cousin-to-be's sonogram was scratchy and dark, with absolutely no contrast. I couldn't help picturing it in a *Highlights* magazine, under the heading, "Can You Find the Hidden Baby?"

Second, the proportions were all off. She reminded me of the wizard's big head in *The Wizard of Oz*.

Not to mention that she was naked and sleeping. I mean, puh-leeze. No privacy whatsoever.

Despite all that, I could hardly keep from crying. Before this baby, my aunt had been through a miscarriage, so we were all a little worried, although we'd tried not to dwell on that too much. Now, after all these months, and all of our dreams and fantasies, we were actually seeing a real, live, almost-born baby. I was so filled with emotion I wanted to burst.

Janine was scrutinizing the fax. "Ariana,"

she announced. "She definitely looks like an Ariana."

"I thought maybe Hideyoshi," Mom said. "That was Mimi's older sister."

Oops. Forget about holding back tears.

At the mention of Mimi's name, my eyes were like Niagara Falls.

Mimi was my grandmother. She was also my favorite person in the whole world. Boy, did I wish she were still alive. She would have been so proud, looking at her new granddaughter.

"How about . . . Mimi?" I suggested, sniffling.

Mom put her arm around my shoulder. Her eyes were pretty misty, too. "That is a beautiful choice for a name."

Little Mimi. The name fit. Our family had lost one member; now we were gaining a new one. Whenever I thought of Mimi, I felt a hole deep inside me. Now, in a funny way, I could feel it starting to fill.

Would my aunt choose that name, too? I hoped so. Mimi was her mom, after all.

But you never knew. Especially with an aunt whose own name is Peaches.

Yes, Peaches.

Don't worry, it's a nickname. Her real name is Miyoshi. My mom's name is Rioko. We're Japanese-Americans. Mimi was Japanese-

Japanese. Which explains the traditional names in my mom's generation and the more Americanized names in mine.

Peaches is a special case. She's a lot younger than my mom, for one thing. Plus she's wild and wacky, which makes her a real oddball in the Kishi family.

I, Claudia, am another oddball. It's nice to have company.

Don't get me wrong. My mom and dad and sister are great. Kind and smart and thoughtful, all of them. But when it comes to fun? Well, let's just say they're — relaxationally challenged.

My dad's idea of a good time is doing the crossword puzzle in the Sunday *New York Times*. He's a partner in an investment firm, and his eyes light up when he talks about stocks and bonds (which to me sound like old-fashioned torture instruments). My mom's a librarian. She believes I should read only classic literature, so I have to hide my Nancy Drew books (which I love and she hates).

In my parents' eyes, Janine is perfection. She finishes my dad's puzzles after he gives up. She not only likes classical books, but classical music and classical clothes. That day, for example, she was wearing a prim, button-down white shirt with a pin in the shape of a profile of Bach.

Whoever that is.

Janine's in high school, but she's smarter than some of the teachers, so she takes classes at the local university (in Stoneybrook, Connecticut, where we live). She studies subjects such as calculus and physics.

Me? I thought physics was the study of how to put bubbles in soda. (Say it aloud and you'll know what I'm talking about.) I'm also allergic to spelling and crossword puzzles. My grades, as you can guess, are pretty rotten.

It's not easy being Janine's younger sister. At the beginning of every school year, my teachers all think I'm acting stupid on purpose. Then, when they realize I'm not an academic genius, they take weeks to recover from the disappointment.

Except my art teachers. They adore me. I am absolutely passionate about art. I love to sculpt, paint, draw, and make jewelry. I look at everything with an artist's eye: in terms of light, color, and texture. I collect all kinds of stuff, materials to use in collages and interesting clothes from thrift shops and yard sales. Once, when I was wearing a really wild outfit, my friend Abby Stevenson told me I use my body as a canvas.

I thought that was hilarious. I repeated it to my family over dinner. My mom smiled politely, Janine shrugged, and my dad became very grim. He thought it was an insult.

Honestly, sometimes I think I was switched with another baby at birth.

Just sometimes. Mimi understood my artistic side. And Peaches' sense of humor is a lot like mine. I think I inherited her genes.

And you know what? Little Mimi was going to inherit them, too. I just knew it.

"Well," Dad said, turning away from the fax machine, "what a terrific way to start the day."

"Can I keep this?" I asked, holding up the fax paper.

"Maybe you can colorize it," Janine suggested with a smile. "Like those old movies."

"Cool," I said. (Yes, sometimes Janine does have good ideas.)

I brought the fax paper to the kitchen table and propped it up against the salt and pepper shakers. Dad and Mom were already pouring skim milk over their favorite cereal, Puke Nuggets. (The real name is Pure Nuggets, but they have about ninety-three different grains, no sugar, and no taste. Plus they're dark brown. Looking at them makes me sick.) Janine fixed herself some oatmeal and sat down with a list of four hundred or so vocabulary words to memorize for French class.

I popped a couple of frozen waffles in the

toaster, slathered butter on them, and gave them a maple syrup bath.

Now, that's a breakfast.

Oh. Another big difference between me and the rest of the family is that I *love* sweets.

I don't know why I don't weigh three hundred pounds. Just my metabolism, I guess. Everybody warns me that it's harder to keep weight off when you're older. Which just means I'll have to stuff my face now while I have the chance.

Keeping that in mind, I snuck three chocolate chip cookies while I was clearing the breakfast table.

After breakfast I folded up the fax, put it in my backpack, and headed out the door for school. " 'Bye!" I called over my shoulder.

" 'Bye!" Mom and Dad called back.

"Au revoir, Claudia!" shouted Janine, pronouncing my name "Clohdia."

(Gag *moi*.)

As I walked outside, I sniffed deeply. Our neighbors have a wisteria vine that blooms every year in May.

Have you ever smelled wisteria? You must. To me, that smell *is* spring. I hurried down the sidewalk, humming to myself. I began to imagine what it would be like to push Little Mimi down the same street in a stroller. I would definitely stop and hold her up to the wisteria blossoms. I read somewhere that babies are deeply affected by their experiences right after birth. So maybe throughout her whole life she'd remember that first, fragrant, beautiful spring with her favorite cousin.

I started to cry again as I turned left onto Elm Street.

As usual, Stacey McGill, Mary Anne Spier, and Mallory Pike were all waiting for me at the corner of Elm and Burnt Hill Road.

The very first thing Mary Anne said was, "Are you all right?"

I wiped away a tear. "I'm fine," I replied, reaching into my backpack for the fax. "Meet my new cousin."

Guess what? Not one of them said Little Mimi looked compressed. They all agreed she was the world's cutest almost-baby.

My friends are so great.

We oohed and aahed all the way to Fawcett Avenue, where we met Jessi Ramsey. Her comment about Little Mimi? "She has the most beautiful fingers."

It was true. You could barely see them, just to the right of Little Mimi's cheek. But they were so thin and delicate-looking.

Jessi waltzed with the fax, cradling it in her arms and spinning around. (That's Jessi. She's dance-obsessed.)

As we were walking past Brenner Field, she did a big, flashy turn. My cousin flew out of her hands.

I thought I would have a heart attack. I raced after the fax, which was blowing away on a gust of wind.

Out of the corner of my eye, I spotted Logan Bruno running toward us across the field. He's Mary Anne's boyfriend, and he also happens to be a football, baseball, and track team member, so he's fast. And strong.

I was almost flattened.

He snatched the paper off the ground and looked at it. "Whoa, what's this? Some kind of underwater fungus?"

Underwater fungus?

I grabbed it out of his hands. "That, for your information," I snapped, "is my cousin."

"Oh! Sorry."

"*Lo*gan," Mary Anne said disapprovingly.

The rest of the way to school, Logan acted like a puppy dog with its tail between its legs.

In school, my good mood just became better and better. First of all, I almost flunked a math quiz. (Why is that good? I didn't say I *flunked* it, did I?) Second, I hadn't finished the reading assignment in English, but the teacher didn't even call on me once.

I felt like a major dork in social studies,

though, when my teacher, Ms. Bernhardt, asked, "Who can identify the City of Brotherly Love . . . Claudia?"

Huh?

I thought fast. Brotherville? Nahh. It was probably a name based on some other language. What was the Spanish word for brother? I knew it once . . . *hermano*. (Yes!) Was there an Hermanotown? . . . Hermano City? . . .

Suddenly it hit me. I remembered a city name on a freeway sign in Southern California. It was awhile ago, when I was visiting my friend, Dawn Schafer.

"Any ideas?" Ms. Bernhardt pressed.

I cleared my throat. "Hermosa Beach?"

Ms. Bernhardt looked at me as if I'd just sprouted antennae. Then she burst out laughing so hard she almost fell off her high heels. "*Hermosa Beach?* Dear lord, where did you come up with that, honey?"

(Ms. Bernhardt talks like that. She's one-of-a-kind in our school. Well, two of a kind, actually. She and Ms. Vandela are the only SMS teachers who wear heels and Big Hair and Major Makeup. We call them Dolly One and Dolly Two, because they both look like the singer Dolly Parton.)

"Well, uh, I guess it's not, huh?" I mumbled. (I know. What a genius.)

Behind me, I could hear the unmistakable giggling of Grace Blume, contender for Most Obnoxious Student of the Year.

In the seat next to mine, Melissa Banks (who's no picnic herself) whirled around angrily toward Grace. "Ssssh!"

"Maybe you can enlighten us, Grace," Ms. Bernhardt said.

Silence.

"I'll give you a hint," Ms. Bernhardt continued. Then, in an exaggerated voice, she said, "This is *social studies* class. And we've been studying the *United States Constitution*."

"Washington?" Grace asked timidly.

"Philadelphia!" I blurted out.

"Bingo!" Ms. Bernhardt said. "Pass Go, collect two hundred dollars! From the Greek — *philos* for love, *adelphos* for brother." She opened her desk drawer. "Now, Claudia, you can choose what's inside drawer number one or settle for the tremendous praise you just received from your favorite teacher."

I pretended to think hard. "I'll take the drawer."

Ms. Bernhardt pulled out a glossy travel brochure that said *Philadelphia* on it.

"You have won an all-expenses paid trip for both my social studies classes, exactly two weeks from this Friday, for an entire weekend, to the City of Brotherly Love, for the purpose of studying American history firsthand."

"Yeeeeeeaaa!" Melissa jumped out of her seat and started hugging me.

Sometimes Melissa can be a little . . . excitable. But I didn't mind. I was psyched.

Ms. Bernhardt had said both of her classes would go. Stacey and Abby were in her other class. So they'd be invited, too.

Whoa. My first glimpse of Little Mimi, a passing grade in math, and a trip to Philadelphia with two of my best friends.

I was on a roll.

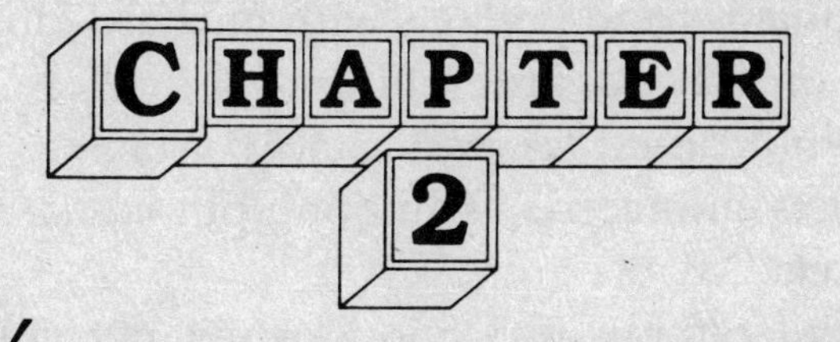

"You're going on a trip to *Philadelphia?*" Kristy Thomas said with a funny look.

"Isn't that cool?" I asked.

"I guess," Kristy replied. "I mean, it's not, like, Disneyland or anything."

"The Liberty Bell is there," Mary Anne pointed out.

Kristy did not look impressed. "Uh-huh, what else?"

Abby Stevenson leaped up and began dancing around my bedroom, singing the *Rocky* theme and pumping her fists in the air. "The place with the steps," she said. "You know, where *Rocky* was made."

"The Philadelphia Museum of Art," I interjected. "And down the street from it is the Rodin Museum, with all his sculptures."

"Who's Row Dan?" Kristy asked.

"R-O-D-I-N," I said. "It's a French name."

"Excuuuse me," Kristy said with a huff.

"Great food, too," Stacey piped up. "Cheesesteaks and hoagies and pretzels with mustard — "

Now Abby started singing, "Cheesesteaks and hoagies and pretzels with mustard" to the tune of "My Favorite Things."

"Who turned *her* on?" Stacey asked.

Kristy grimaced. "You don't put *mustard* on pretzels."

I slid off my bed and opened my closet. Reaching behind my shoe boxes, I pulled out a box of jumbo-size hard pretzels I'd stashed there. "Let's try it. I'll get some mustard from the kitchen."

Kristy glanced at my clock, which said 5:28. "You have two minutes."

"Yikes." I sprinted out.

Believe me, with Kristy Thomas as president, you do not enter a Baby-sitters Club meeting late. I'm lucky. My bedroom is club headquarters, so I usually don't have to worry. But boy, did I fly down to the kitchen.

Kristy's actually a sweet person, under all that bossiness. She has incredible energy, too, and she's super smart. Not Janine-Kishi-Mega-IQ smart, but problem-solving, people-organizing smart.

The Baby-sitters Club was Kristy's idea. She thought of it one day when her mom was having trouble finding a sitter for Kristy's little brother, David Michael. As Mrs. Thomas called all over Stoneybrook in vain, Kristy's Idea Engine chugged into high gear.

Here's how the club works. We have nine members, seven regulars and two associates. We meet three times a week (in my room), on Mondays, Wednesdays, and Fridays, from five-thirty to six o'clock. Stoneybrook parents call during those times to book baby-sitting jobs.

Simple and convenient. Our clients always find a terrific sitter, and we sitters can count on pretty steady jobs. We try to share the work equally, which means we can't promise our clients one regular sitter. But we keep each other informed about our charges' habits, preferences, and needs. In fact, Kristy requires us to write about all our jobs in the official BSC notebook. Our clients eventually meet us all, and they get used to our system.

Kristy is a perfect president. She runs the meetings and makes sure we stick to business. Whenever our charges need some extra-special treatment, she comes up with great ideas. She organized a softball team for little kids. She invented Kid-Kits, boxes full of old toys, games, and art supplies, which we sometimes take to our jobs.

To Kristy, everything is an opportunity for advertising. Forget about trying to carry on a conversation with her in a crowd. The minute a family walks by, *zoom*, Kristy is after them with a sales pitch and a flier. It is so embarrassing, but hey, it works.

Kristy can zoom around pretty well. She's really athletic — short and wiry and very coordinated. She has shoulder-length brown hair, and she always dresses in casual clothes. (I've tried to convince her to think more about her image, but does she listen? Noooo.)

For most of our lives, Kristy lived across the street from me. When we were little, her dad walked out on the family, leaving Mrs. Thomas to raise four kids on her own, including David Michael, who was just a baby. (Kristy has two older brothers, fifteen-year-old Sam and seventeen-year-old Charlie.)

For years, Mrs. Thomas held the family together by herself. Then she married a very rich guy named Watson Brewer, and Kristy and her family moved into his mansion (far away from me . . . sigh). Watson and Kristy's mom adopted a two-year-old Vietnamese girl, whose name is Emily Michelle. Then Kristy's grandmother, Nannie, moved in. She helps take care of Emily. Watson's two kids from a previous marriage, Andrew (who's four) and Karen (seven), live in the house during alternate months.

Add to that a whole zoo's worth of pets,

and it's a pretty crowded place, even for a mansion.

Because Kristy's new neighborhood is so distant, Charlie has to drive her to BSC meetings. Despite that, she's never been late.

That Wednesday, I was about to be. And I *live* in BSC headquarters.

I dashed into my room, holding a bottle of mustard, just as Kristy belted out, "I call this meeting to order!"

I leaped onto my bed.

"Who has the pretzels?" I asked.

Crunch, crunch, crunch. Six silent moving jaws answered me.

Stacey held up an almost-empty bag. I pulled out a pretzel and squirted mustard all over it.

"Philadelphia, here I come," I said, inserting it into my mouth.

"How is it?" Mallory asked.

I chewed thoughtfully for a moment. "I don't see what the big deal is."

"I think you're supposed to use soft pretzels," Stacey said.

"*Now* you tell me."

Rrrrring!

I picked up the receiver. "Hello, Baby-sitters Club, Claudia speaking." (My mustard breath bounced back at me. Boy, was I glad smell doesn't transmit over phone lines.)

"Hello, Claudia, it's Linda Arnold. I know it's short notice, but do you have anyone available for Friday night?"

"I'll check and call you right back," I replied.

I said good-bye, hung up, and gave the information to Mary Anne.

That's our procedure. As secretary, Mary Anne keeps the record book, which contains a calendar of all our jobs. She needs to know everyone's availability for each day, so she marks the calendar with all our conflicts: doctor and dentist appointments, after-school lessons, family trips, and so on. In the back of the book she maintains an up-to-date list of client names and addresses, the rates they pay, and the ages and special interests of their kids.

"Uh-oh," Mary Anne said. "Abby's going to a show that night, Claud's at the Prezziosos', Stacey's going to New York, and Kristy and I are having pizza night with our families."

"What about Shannon?" Jessi asked.

"Debate team practice." Mary Anne reached for the phone. "I'll call Logan."

She tapped out her boyfriend's number, and within minutes we had a sitter for the Arnolds for Friday night.

Good system, huh?

By the way, in case you're wondering, I'm

the BSC's vice-president. I have three jobs: (1) answering all the calls that come in during nonmeeting hours, (2) hosting all the meetings, and (3) providing the junk food (believe me, I have much more than just pretzels stashed away).

What I do is nothing compared to what Mary Anne does. Her middle name is Organized. (Mine is Chaotic. You should see my room.)

Mary Anne also used to live across the street from me, in the house next to Kristy's. What a threesome we were. Mom says that when we were little, Kristy would build towers out of blocks, Mary Anne would sort them by size and color, and I would try to eat them. That pretty much sums us up.

None of us ever knew Mrs. Spier. She died when Mary Anne was a baby. Mr. Spier raised Mary Anne with tons of rules. She had a super-early curfew and had to wear pigtailed hair and little-girl dresses to school. Forget about getting her ears pierced. The trouble was, Mary Anne was too sweet and shy to complain, so it took awhile for her dad to realize she needed to grow up.

Mary Anne's life changed a lot when Dawn Schafer moved to Stoneybrook from California and joined the BSC. Dawn and Mary Anne discovered that Dawn's mom (who was divorced) had grown up here and had been Mr. Spier's high school girlfriend. So guess who ended up reuniting, dating, and marrying? (With a little help from matchmakers Mary Anne and Dawn.)

The Schafers lived in a rambling, two-hundred-year-old farmhouse, so Mary Anne and her dad moved in with them. Dawn has since moved back to California to live with her dad and brother, and boy, do we miss her.

Mary Anne wears normal clothes now, and a pretty cool, short hairstyle. She looks a little like Kristy, short and brown-haired. In fact, Kristy and Mary Anne are best friends — although you'd never mistake one for the other. Mary Anne's quiet and sensitive and thoughtful. She's also a top-notch crier. Mention the word "wedding" and watch the mist start to form. Logan always teases her for blubbering at movies. (But let's face it, he loves it. The sadder the movie, the more she snuggles with him.)

If Mary Anne wins the BSC Most Sensitive award, Stacey nails down the Most Unique (nosing out yours truly, I think). Why? Top of the list: she likes *math*. Because of that rare quality, she's the BSC treasurer. On Mondays she collects dues, which the club uses for special events, advertising, my phone bill, and gas money for Charlie Thomas.

Stacey's my best friend. She's also the only BSC member to hail from New York City. Personally, I think NYC is the coolest place in the world. You could spend months just going from one art gallery to the next. Stacey spent her whole life there, until her dad's company transferred him to Connecticut. That was when she joined the BSC. But she wasn't here long, because the company made him move back to New York again. Well, all the moving must have worn down her parents' marriage, which wasn't doing too well anyway. All of a sudden we heard that they were divorcing, and Stacey was moving back to Stoneybrook with her mom. (She actually turned down the opportunity to stay in the Big Apple with her dad. Why? Because of her great friends here, of course.)

You would recognize Stacey instantly at a BSC meeting. She's the only one with blonde hair, and the only one who turns down sweets. Stacey has a condition called diabetes. If she eats too much sugar, she could go into a coma. She can lead a normal life as long as she eats regular, sugar-free meals and injects herself daily with a hormone called insulin. I have seen her do this, and it is not disgusting at all. (Well, not very.)

Stacey may be good in math, but her passion is fashion. She dresses cool, sleek, and urban.

She can predict what the next hot look is going to be, weeks in advance. I guess she picked up that talent while living all those years near New York City boutiques.

Too bad Stacey didn't know Abigail Stevenson back then. They might have spotted each other on those crowded Manhattan streets. Abby's a former Long Islander and frequent NYC visitor.

Abby and her twin sister, Anna, grew up near the beach, and their mom commuted to her job with a publishing company in the Big Apple. (Their dad died in a car accident when they were nine, but they don't talk about that much.) Abby's our alternate officer, which means she takes over the duties of any regular officer who might be absent.

Dawn Schafer used to be our alternate. After she moved to California, we tried to function with just six regular members. It was a nightmare. We became so busy, some of us were doing two jobs in a day. We came very close to needing to turn down work (which would have given Kristy a heart attack).

Imagine the look on Kristy's face the day Abby and Anna moved into a house down the street from the Brewer mansion. Not one, but two thirteen-year-old girls with great personalities! I'm surprised Kristy didn't drag them by the hair to a meeting.

Actually, in a nice, civilized way, we offered both sisters membership. Anna Stevenson turned us down, though, mostly because she's a serious musician who practices all the time.

So Abby became our new alternate officer. And boy, are we glad. She's outgoing and hilarious. You would not believe her imitations. She impersonated *me* once, gabbing away with a mouthful of caramels while wrapping her hair in twist-ties. I almost died from laughing so hard.

Abby has the world's most gorgeous hair. It's a deep, luscious brown, so thick and curly it falls in ringlets to her shoulders. She has to work hard to put it into a ponytail for sports. (She's an amazing natural athlete, which made Kristy a little jealous at first.)

Like Stacey, Abby has a serious health condition. Abby's is asthma (plus about a million allergies). She keeps an inhaler with her at all times.

Now you know all our regular officers. Jessi and Mallory are our junior officers because they're eleven and in sixth grade (the rest of us are thirteen and in eighth grade), and their parents won't let them baby-sit at night.

How do they feel about this? *Furious* is the closest word. They both think their parents treat them too strictly. Mal calls it "the oldest child syndrome." She says younger siblings are treated much more leniently. (I wish she'd talk to my parents about this.)

Jessi and Mal are best friends. Total horse lovers, too — they talk about *Saddle Club* characters as if they're real people. Mallory wants to be a writer/illustrator of children's books and create a horse series of her own someday.

Maybe she'd be better off writing a sitcom about a humongous family. Mallory has seven younger siblings. Sitting for them takes two BSC members (a traffic cop would be nice, too). Mal has thick, reddish-brown hair and pale skin, and she wears glasses and braces (which she hates).

Jessi has an eight-year-old sister and an almost two-year-old brother. Her family moved to Stoneybrook from Oakley, New Jersey. There, the Ramseys were one of many African-American families. Here, though, they are in a small minority, and I'm embarrassed to say that some Stoneybrookites were awful to them at first. (I've felt prejudice here myself, so I really sympathized.)

Our two associate members aren't required to attend meetings or pay dues. They take up slack when we're extra-busy. Logan is one of them. He's a great sitter. He has a killer smile, blondish-brown hair, and a slight Southern accent (he's from Louisville, Kentucky).

Our other associate is Shannon Kilbourne.

She goes to a private school called Stoneybrook Day School, where she's in the Honor Society and about a million other clubs. Even so, she usually finds time to sit when we need her.

As you can tell from our close call with the Arnolds, we are a hot ticket in Stoneybrook. One more call for Friday night and we'd be stuck.

The phone did ring three more times during the meeting. The first two calls were jobs for the upcoming week.

The third call came while everyone was preparing to leave, just before six o'clock.

"Hello, Baby-sitters Club," I said.

"Claudia?"

I didn't recognize the voice at first. It sounded male and young, but not like any of the dads who call us.

"Yes?"

"Heyyyyy, it's thaaaaat time!" the voice said, sounding like a game show host.

My mind flashed an Alan Gray Alert. Alan is the Crème de la Creeps of SMS, and phone pranks are his great love.

"If this is you, Alan, we're not — "

"Claudia, it's Russ! I'm about to take Peaches to the hospital."

My heart almost burst out of my chest. "Wha — is it — you mean, *now*?"

"We think so. The contractions are regular enough. Listen, Claudia, I called your parents' number and left a message on the machine. But I figured I'd catch you in person — "

"Yeah! I mean, okay. I mean, go! What are you talking to me for?"

Russ laughed. "Next time we see you, there'll be three of us. 'Bye!"

"I can't wait! 'Bye!"

I hung up the phone.

And then I screamed my lungs out.

"EEEEEEEEEEEEEEEE!"

"What happened?" Stacey asked.

"EEEEEEEEEEEEEEEE!"

"Claudia, calm down!" Kristy screamed.

"That was Russ," I told them. "He's taking Peaches to the hospital right now!"

"Yeeaaaaa!" My friends wrapped me in a great big hug.

Except Abby. She looked confused. "Taking peaches to the hospital? Is this some kind of ancient birthing ritual?"

"Peaches is my aunt," I explained.

"Oh!"

Abby joined the hugfest. Everyone started talking at once:

"Take a camera!"

"Take a camcorder!"

"Bring her warm clothes!"

"Give her a kiss from us!"

"Give her our flier!" (That was Kristy.)

"Call us the *minute* she has the baby!"

We gabbed all the way downstairs. Then we hugged again and said good-bye.

I waved to my friends as they walked away, shouting instructions to me.

I shut the door and raced to the phone. I called Mom's and Dad's offices, but they'd both left already.

When I hung up, I didn't know what to do with myself. My legs took me to the right. Then they shifted and took me to the left. I rearranged furniture. I bit my nails.

Thoughts tumbled through my mind.

I could run to the hospital.

Nahhh, it was too far. Besides, my parents would be home soon, and I was sure Russ wanted me to tell them in person.

But what if Little Mimi were born while I was waiting? What if Dad hit a lot of traffic? What about Janine? Mom was supposed to pick her up from the community college on her way home. What if Janine were in the middle of discovering a new theory of physics, and the teachers wouldn't let her leave?

I must have looked at the living room clock a million times. It was moving so slowly, I thought it had broken.

When I heard my dad's car pull up in the driveway, I nearly died.

I ran into the front screen door. Yes, *into*. I forgot to reach for the knob.

By the time I fumbled with the knobs and pushed the door open, Dad had driven inside the garage. I raced around the side of the house and saw him climbing out of the car.

"Get back in!" I called out. "Start it up! We have to go!"

Dad looked at me blankly. Now I could hear Mom's car rolling up the driveway behind me.

I turned around. Mom and Janine were sitting in the front seat. "Stop! Back up! Peaches is having the baby!"

Dad gasped. "They called?"

"Russ did!" I was screaming now, turning my head from Mom's car to Dad's. *"A long time ago! They're probably there already! The baby might be born!"*

Mom blew her horn. I don't know why, probably out of joy or excitement, but it made me nearly jump out of my clothes.

As she backed into the street, I ran to Dad's car and climbed in.

I have never seen Dad back up so fast. The engine was whining. "How far along is she?" he asked.

"Oak Street, if they had a late start," I said. "But they're probably — "

"I mean, in terms of the birth! Has the baby dropped?"

"Dropped what?"

"Never mind!"

We were already on the street and straightening out.

We followed Mom and Janine to the hospital. I know, I know, we should have all gone in one car. But we were beyond bananas. No one thought about it.

We tore into the parking lot of Stoneybrook General Hospital. Mom found a parking space near ours, and the four of us dashed for the main entrance.

"How close is she?" Mom asked.

"I don't know," I replied.

"What room is she in?" Janine asked.

"I don't know."

I must have said "I don't know" about five more times before we reached the reception desk.

The nurse sent us to the maternity wing, on the fourth floor.

I had never seen so many red eyes in my life as I saw there. Dads paced wearily in the hallways. New moms in hospital gowns shuffled slowly in and out of their rooms, supported by husbands, friends, and parents. It seemed as if the whole floor was having a massive Bad Hair Day.

Me? I wanted to cry.

From happiness.

You cannot imagine the joy in the air of a maternity wing unless you've been there. It seems to float around everybody like a huge shimmering light. Inside everybody, too. You see it behind the spidery veins in the eyes. You see it in all the sagging faces and stooped, exhausted postures.

You know that none of those people would want to be anywhere else in the world.

I saw a teeny little baby, fast asleep, being rolled into a room in a bassinet. And a split second later I heard a burst of laughing and cooing and crying.

I nearly lost it.

I nearly lost my family, too. They were gone when I turned around.

"Mom?" I called out.

Mom peered from around a corner. "This way!"

I followed her to another desk. Behind it was a nurse, wearing a green outfit and a mask and a green plastic hat that looked like a shower cap. She and Dad were scanning a clipboard together.

Overhead, a sign that said *Delivery* pointed down the hallway.

"Miyoshi Benedict?" the nurse said. "She's in delivery right now with her husband. If you'll take a seat in our lounge, I'll let them know you're here . . ."

Delivery.

I know this sounds stupid, but I thought the sign was pointing to the mailroom. Duh. *Delivery* meant *baby* delivery!

Peaches was in there. Beyond the sign. About to give birth.

"You made it!"

I turned at the sound of my uncle Russ's voice. He had on a green outfit just like the nurse's.

He wasn't wearing a mask, probably because they could not find one big enough to fit over his smile.

Mom, Janine, and I hugged him and Dad pumped his hand.

"So?" Mom said. "What's the news?"

"She's only about a centimeter," Russ replied. "But the head is down and the fetal monitor's strong, so if the dilation doesn't increase they may induce with Pitocin."

Oh.

Right.

I nodded and pretended I understood.

"In other words," Russ said, "it may be awhile, folks."

"That's okay," I blurted out. "We'll wait."

"I'll tell Peaches you're here," Russ said.

"Thanks," Mom said.

"Keep us posted," Janine called out.

We walked away from the desk. The waiting

room was a small alcove just outside the maternity wing. Inside were two plastic-upholstered sofas, a magazine rack, a candy and soda machine (dinner!), and a pay phone. No windows, though, and no artwork.

Dad and Janine sat. Mom and I paced.

And paced.

And paced.

When Russ poked his head in, I spun around so fast I knocked the phone receiver off the hook.

"Peaches wants to see you," Russ said to Mom.

"Is she—?" I squeaked.

Russ shook his head. "Not yet. She just needs a little TLC."

That was a phrase I understood. Mom bustled out, a huge smile on her face.

I kept pacing. Janine was doing physics homework. Dad was reading the same page of the *Wall Street Journal* over and over. I grew so tired of pacing I sat down and started reading a magazine, cover to cover.

"Popular Mechanics?" Janine asked.

Oh. I hadn't any idea what I'd been looking at.

After a while, we were all yawning.

Janine finally asked, "Claudia, when Russ called, did he *tell* you to rush over?"

"Well, no," I replied.

"Then why were you in such a hurry?"

"Ja*nine,* he said she was going to the hospital. You go to the hospital when you're about to have a baby! How was I to know that — "

"Okay, okay, it's an understandable mistake. So why don't we go home and wait until — "

"Go home? How could you think of — "

"Ssssh, please," Dad said.

Then Mom walked back in, and we all fell silent.

She looked tired. "They're going to induce," she told us.

"Is that bad?" I asked.

Mom shook her head. "It means they're giving her medication to speed things along, that's all."

Speed things along? That was good news.

I was halfway through the *American Medical Journal* when I heard a commotion near the nurse's desk. Then I thought I heard Peaches. Moaning.

I ran out to see two nurses wheeling Peaches, on a rolling bed, toward a pair of white, swinging doors. Russ was jogging alongside.

"Dr. Zuckerman to delivery, please," a voice blared over a loudspeaker. "Stat."

From behind us, a doctor walked briskly out of the maternity area. He ducked behind the nurses's desk, put on a shower cap and a green space suit, and went into the delivery room.

I squeezed Janine's hand. I felt as if I'd swallowed a beach ball.

"Come," Dad said. "Let's sit down."

He put his arm around Mom's shoulder, and we all walked back into the waiting room.

"How long will it be?" I asked.

"Soon," Mom said. "Very soon."

I was a train wreck. I couldn't sit. I couldn't read.

Soon? *Soon* felt like a thousand years.

I thought Russ would never come. I thought he'd forgotten about us. I imagined us sitting there, neglected, gathering dust, until Little Mimi was ready for grade school.

And then, just when I thought I would pass out from the tension, Russ ran into the room. His eyes were glazed, his smile so bright we could have seen him in the dark.

"Claudia, Janine," he announced, "you have a new cousin."

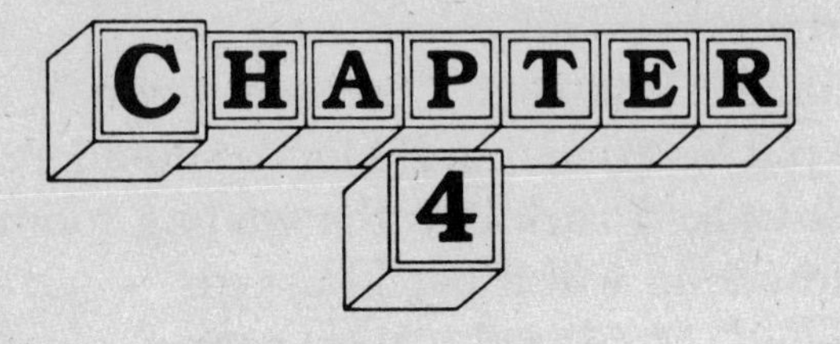

"I do — she's here — what — yaaaahhhh-hooooo!"

I jumped on Russ. Unfortunately, Janine and Mom were already smothering him with hugs.

I slid off. Next to me, Dad was beaming. So I jumped on him.

I was so excited I almost forgot the most important question. "What's her name?" I quickly asked.

Mimi. Mimi. Mimi. Mimi . . . I tried to send telepathic signals.

"Lynn," Russ replied with a big smile. "After Claudia Lynn Kishi."

Well, I let out a sob so loud, I thought I'd wake up all the sleeping babies in the hospital. Russ wrapped me in his arms and said, "It was Peaches' idea. She insisted on it."

"Oh . . ." I said. "Oh . . ." (It was the only word I could think of at the time.)

"I wanted the name Agnes," Russ said with a sigh. "But I gave in at the last minute."

Dad howled with laughter. I bopped Russ on the arm.

"She's okay?" Mom asked.

"Ten toes, ten fingers," Russ replied. "And a powerful cry."

Mom smiled. "I meant Peaches."

"So did I," Russ shot back.

"What's she look like?" Janine asked. "I mean, the baby."

"Uh, sort of like this." Russ squinched up his eyes and opened his mouth into a silent howl.

"I recognize that look," Mom said. "Pure Peaches."

"Can we see her?" Janine asked.

Russ shook his head. "Not tonight. It's too late. Peaches told me to say she loves you all but she's exhausted and hopes you understand."

"Can we come tomorrow after school?" I asked.

"You better," Russ answered. "By then we'll need a trained baby-sitter."

I love Russ. He is so cool.

We said good-byes and exchanged more hugs.

I floated all the way to the car.

When we arrived home and I saw the clock

in the living room, I could not believe my eyes. It was ten forty-five. I ran to the phone.

"What are you doing?" Mom asked.

"Calling my friends," I replied. "I promised."

"Not at this hour," Dad said. "They can wait."

Grrrrr.

That night I could not sleep. I tried and tried, but my smile was keeping me awake.

Yes, I'm serious. Every time I started dozing off, I'd think of the next day, and *sproooiiingg,* my cheeks would start to hurt.

In the morning, I raced downstairs and wolfed down my cereal. I wanted to call Stacey so badly, but Mom was on the phone to Peaches in the hospital. Afterward she reported that Peaches and Lynn were happy and resting, and they could hardly wait for our visits.

"I know! I could stop off there before school," I suggested. "I wouldn't be too late."

Mom quickly flushed that idea. Sigh.

I decided to skip the phone calling. I'd tell everybody in person.

I was the first to arrive at the corner of Elm Street and Burnt Hill Road. The moment Stacey spotted me from up the street, she ran.

"So?" was her breathless greeting.

"She's Lynn!" I blurted out.

"Little Mimi?"

"Yes!"

Stacey shrieked. "Yeeeaaaa! Why didn't you call?"

I explained everything. Minute by minute.

Then, when Mary Anne arrived, I repeated the whole story. And again when Mallory ran up. And one more time for Jessi, a block later. We were so loud, I'm surprised the neighbors didn't start throwing things at us.

"When are you going to see her?" Jessi asked as we walked toward SMS.

"After school."

"Take a camera," Mallory suggested.

"A Polaroid," Stacey added. "So we can see right away."

"Call us," Jessi said.

"Which gift will you bring her?" Mary Anne asked.

"Maybe the diaper wraps," I said. "I was going to give them to Peaches at the shower, but I gave her the picture frames and the crib bumpers instead. I also made this cool mobile with figures in black-and-white because that helps newborns' eyes to focus. Oh! And a fairy tale painting, with all my favorite characters — "

Jessi burst out laughing. "How many presents do you have?"

"I didn't count," I replied. "They're all

tucked away at home. Ugh. I hope I haven't forgotten any of them."

"How about the blanket?" Mary Anne asked softly. "Do you still have it?"

I had almost forgotten. During Peaches' first pregnancy, Mary Anne and I had started knitting a lavender crib blanket for the baby. (Mary Anne had done most of the work at first. She's a talented knitter.) After the miscarriage, I had finished it and put it away in the back of my closet, just in case.

Now, just-in-case was about to be a reality.

I smiled at Mary Anne. "I sure do. *That's* what I'll bring."

A moment later, Logan came bounding toward us. I have to admit, telling the news the fourth time around was every bit as much fun as the first.

Logan's response? "Does she look like the fax?"

Boys.

As you can imagine, that school day was not on my list of all-time greatest learning experiences. Normally my teachers think I'm in a fog. That day, they were trying to find me in the asteroid belt.

I just could not stop thinking about Lynn. I was missing her first day. I would never know what she looked like as a new newborn. I might have lost out on that important initial bonding time.

Chill, I kept telling myself.

I counted the minutes to the end of school. I couldn't even pay attention in social studies, when Ms. Bernhardt was telling us about our weekend in Philadelphia.

After school I burst like a cannonball out the front door. I practically ran all the way home.

Mom and Dad were still at work, and Janine was in math club or something equally thrilling. I let myself in, scooted upstairs, and pulled open the door of my closet.

The blanket was wrapped in paper that I had decorated with drawings of rattles, fairy-tale characters, blocks, and little babies. I stuffed the package in my backpack.

Zoom. I was outside, on my bike, and on the way to Stoneybrook General.

I parked my bike at a rack. Then I ran to the front desk and ripped off my bike helmet, panting for breath. My hair must have looked like a haystack. "Benedict . . . maternity . . . Peaches?" I gasped.

Yes, the receptionist did understand me, somehow. "Room four-thirty-five. Use the rear elevator."

"Thanks!" I darted away. I waited about

three hundred hours for the elevator. I rode up, squished between two doctors, and ran off at the fourth floor.

I headed straight for the delivery area.

"Excuse me, miss?" an urgent voice called out. "You can't go there!"

I turned to see a nurse rushing toward me. "But — my aunt — the baby —" I stammered.

She smiled. "You want maternity. It's around the corner."

"Thanks!"

I took a deep breath. I composed myself in a mirror by the elevator. I removed my backpack and took out the gift.

And then I tore off down the hall.

Room 435 was the third door. "Hi, Pea — !" I began.

I stopped myself. Peaches was fast asleep. Around her, flower arrangements were perched on every flat surface.

I backed out. Peaches had been through a lot, and I didn't want to disturb her.

But when was I going to see Lynn?

"Psssst! Claudia!"

I whirled around.

Uncle Russ was walking toward me from the other end of the hall, wearing a yellow apron. In his arms was a teeny bundle of blankets.

I rushed up to him. "Hi! I brought you a —"

"Shhhh!" he replied.

He tilted the bundle toward me. Inside a little opening at the top of the bundle, I caught my first glimpse of my cousin.

I opened my mouth to say something, but no words came out. Nothing could describe how beautiful she was. How serene and perfect. Her eyes were closed but somehow she radiated life and energy. Her hair was jet-black and spiky, sticking straight up.

Not only was she gorgeous, she was cool. A chip off the old block.

"May I hold her?" I asked, handing him my gift.

"Sure," Russ said.

I was amazed at how light she was, even with all the blankets. "Hi, Lynnie-Lynn," I said, through sniffles of joy.

We walked back into Peaches' room. The moment Russ sat on the bed, Peaches began to waken.

"We have a visitor," he said softly.

Peaches broke into a huge smile. "What do you think, Claudia?"

"I think she's stunning!" I said.

"She likes you," Peaches replied. "I can tell."

"How? She's sleeping!"

Peaches shrugged. "She was sleeping when

your mom took her, but she burst out crying."

"Mom was here?"

"On her lunch break. She couldn't keep herself away."

I gave Lynn a kiss. "Everybody loves you soooo much!"

Lynn moved. Just a fraction of an inch. And then the corners of her lips turned up.

"She's smiling!" I exclaimed. *"Her very first smile!"*

"I think it's gas," Russ said gently. "Newborns look like that when they have stomach pains."

"But I'm sure she loves your voice," Peaches quickly added.

I nuzzled Lynn a few times. She yawned and her eyes flickered open. They seemed to focus on me for a moment.

Then she burped and fell asleep again.

"Oh, I almost forgot!" I cried. "I have something for you." I handed the gift to my aunt.

"Thank you," Peaches said.

"The paper's great," Russ added.

Peaches carefully peeled back the tape, preserving the paper. When she saw the blanket, her eyes started to water. "You finished it?"

I nodded. That was about all I could do. Looking at Peaches' face, I thought of the only other time I'd seen her cry. It was after her miscarriage, and she had been devastated.

I'd been there at the lowest point of her life. Now I was there at the most glorious. And the blanket kind of brought the two times together.

I dripped a tear of my own, on Lynn's blanket.

Russ handed me a tissue. I cradled Lynn in one arm and wiped my eyes.

"Russ and I have something to ask you, Claudia," Peaches said.

"Sure," I whimpered.

"We've thought about this very carefully, and both of us are in complete agreement," Russ continued.

"Would you be Lynn's godmother?" Peaches asked.

"G-g-godmother?" I stammered.

"We can't think of anyone better suited," Peaches went on. "You'll always have a special place of honor in her life."

I was speechless. Me, cool, calm, never-ruffled Claudia.

Before I dissolved into a puddle, I managed to croak out an answer.

"You bet I will."

FRIDAY

I SAT FOR THE ARNOLD TWINS TONIGHT. I FIGURED, NO PROBLEM. I KNOW THEIR NUMBER. BASICALLY YOU LET THEM ALONE AND ONLY STEP IN IF THEY START TO FIGHT. THEY'RE GOOD KIDS. TOUGH. INDEPENDENT.

AT LEAST, THEY USED TO BE THAT WAY. YOU MAY BE SURPRISED AT THE TWO GIRLS YOU SEE NEXT TIME....

Logan Bruno took homework to the Arnolds' on Friday night.

Don't worry. He was feeling fine. He had not lost his mind. He claims he had a report due on Monday, and he'd been busy with the baseball team for weeks.

I don't know about you, but to me, the idea of doing homework on a Friday night is like going to the beach in a wool suit in August. I'd never dream of it.

But I have to give him the benefit of the doubt. I shouldn't criticize him.

Who knows? Maybe his teacher had offered a cash reward.

Marilyn and Carolyn are eight-year-old, brown-haired, dark-eyed, identical twins. But they're easy to tell apart. Marilyn wears simpler clothes and has shorter hair. Carolyn loves science and can be a little spacey. Marilyn's a musician and very down-to-earth.

The Arnolds were going to a movie that night. As they gave Logan instructions in the kitchen, he could hear Marilyn practicing piano in the living room. Carolyn was in her bedroom, reading.

"Help yourself to a snack," Mr. Arnold said. "The girls seem pretty tired. They said they wanted to watch some TV, which is fine."

"After Marilyn finishes practicing, of

course," Mrs. Arnold added. "And remember, no sweets, no scary movies before bedtime, and if my sister calls, tell her I'll call in the morning."

Everyone said good-bye, and Logan began to spread out his homework on the kitchen table.

The Arnolds' car pulled out of the driveway, and the plinking in the living room suddenly stopped.

"What time is it?" Marilyn called out.

Logan glanced at his watch. "Seven fifty-six," he called back.

Plink, plinkety-plink plink . . .

A few minutes later she yelled, "What time is it now?"

Thump-thump-thump-thump! Before Logan could answer, Carolyn came rushing down the stairs. "Oh, hi, Logan," she said, then dashed toward the living room and called out, "It's eight o'clock!"

The plinking stopped. Marilyn and Carolyn both ran through the kitchen and up the stairs.

"What's up?" Logan asked.

"We're just going to watch TV," Carolyn replied.

"The one in our parents' room," Marilyn explained.

Thump-thump-thump-thump — SLAM!

Up and out of sight. Silence.

Logan smiled. Some sitting job. Piece of cake.

Which reminded him . . . He opened the fridge, took out a snack of pound cake and green grapes, and made himself at home.

He worked for a moment or two, occasionally hearing muffled voices from the TV show upstairs. Funny, he thought. The last time he'd been at the Arnolds', he and the twins had watched a video in the family room.

Was the TV broken? He hoped not. Logan likes to watch the nightly sports report on the news.

He walked into the family room and flicked on the TV. It lit up. In full color. Nice and normal.

"Hey, guys?" he called upstairs. "You don't want to watch down here?"

"That's okay!" Marilyn shouted. "This is fine."

It was fine with Logan, too. He returned to work.

A few minutes later he heard a scream.

He slapped down his pen and ran upstairs. The Arnolds' bedroom door was shut, and from the other side he could hear giggling and whispering.

He opened the door and peeked in. The girls

were calmly lying on the bed, watching an animated tyrannosaur lumber through a forest.

"What happened to the terrible lizards?" a voice intoned. "Let's look at the geological record . . ."

"Everything okay up here?" he asked.

"Great," Marilyn answered.

He headed downstairs, to the sound of crunching dinosaur footsteps.

Back to work. Popping grapes into his mouth, Logan fell deep into his research.

"RRRROOOWWWWWWRRR!"

The sound startled him. Marilyn and Carolyn screamed again, and he heard a thump.

He trudged upstairs again. More giggling and scrambling noises.

Logan poked his head into the room.

The girls were in the same positions. But the dinosaurs were gone. Now Marilyn and Carolyn were watching a basketball game.

"Are you guys *sure* you're okay?" Logan asked.

"Yup," Carolyn answered casually.

Logan sighed and went back downstairs. He figured the girls were channel-surfing to safety from the dinosaurs.

More homework. More snack.

At the third sets of screams, Logan became

suspicious. He ran up again, two steps at a time.

Now a rerun of *The Mary Tyler Moore Show* was playing.

"Uh, I guess Lou was being a little rough in the newsroom?" Logan said.

"Huh?"Carolyn said.

"I mean, you guys sounded pretty scared. Maybe this show is a little mature for you."

Marilyn rolled her eyes. "Lo-*gan* . . . "

"You're not switching channels to something you shouldn't be watching, are you?"

The twins quickly shook their heads.

On the bed was an open TV magazine. Logan scanned the day's listings. The programs on the networks and regular cable stations seemed harmless enough. He skipped over the cable-movie section, because the Arnolds don't subscribe to any of those channels. (The twins love to complain about that.) The dinosaur special was definitely the scariest show.

Logan glanced at the VCR. Could they possibly have sneaked a forbidden video cassette in there? Hmmm . . .

He lumbered downstairs loudly. But this time, when he reached the bottom, he tiptoed back up.

Through the door, Ted Baxter was bragging

on and on about something. When he was finished, the laugh track blared.

And then it suddenly stopped. The next thing Logan heard was deep, gloomy music and the crack of thunder. A quavery female voice asked, "That . . . *thing*. In the bicycle basket. What is it?"

"I don't know," a guy answered. "Looks like a mask or something."

The music became louder.

"It's not a mask," the female said. "It's a . . . a — YEEEEEEAGGGGGGHH!"

The TV character's scream was joined by Marilyn's and Carolyn's. Which were even louder.

Logan pushed open the door.

On the TV screen was a close-up of a bicycle basket in the rain. In it was a . . . well, I don't want to say. It's too gross. Let me put it this way, according to Logan, its expression was not happy.

And the liquid it was floating in was not rain.

Logan almost barfed. He strode into the room, picked up the remote, and pressed Off.

"Heyyyyy!" Marilyn complained.

"You guys aren't supposed to watch scary movies," Logan reminded them.

"That wasn't scary!" Carolyn protested.

"Turn it back on!" Marilyn added.

Logan shook his head. "Sorry, guys, a rule's a rule."

"Party pooper," Marilyn muttered.

"What was that, anyway?" Logan grabbed the guide again.

"The BB Channel," Carolyn said grumpily. "Boxoffice Busters."

"Carolyn, shhh!" Marilyn snapped.

"I thought you didn't get any of the premium stations," Logan said.

"It's a free sneak preview," Carolyn replied. "For two weeks."

Logan read aloud the eight o'clock listing for the BB Channel: " '*Horrorville*: *Head's Up* . . . serial killer stalks suburban New England town. Graphic but stylized violence.' "

"It's not as scary as the one we saw last night!" Carolyn said.

"You watched one of these last night?" Logan asked.

"Until Mom turned it off," Marilyn said sheepishly.

"You'd like this one," Carolyn piped up. "The town was just like Stoneybrook."

"And the girl looked like Mary Anne," Marilyn added.

"Listen," Logan said, "it's already nine o'clock. Let's brush teeth and get ready for bed."

"Ohhhhh," Marilyn groaned.

The twins trudged toward the bathroom. In the hallway Carolyn stopped. The hall was dark; a light glowed faintly from around a corner.

She looked back over her shoulder. "Go ahead."

"You go!" Marilyn retorted.

Logan chuckled. "The movie wasn't that scary, huh?"

He walked ahead of them and turned on a light.

"Could you turn on the bathroom light, too?" Carolyn asked.

He did. The girls came running.

Logan let them wash up. Then they asked him to go to their bedrooms with them.

They put on their pj's in Carolyn's room while Logan waited patiently outside the closed door.

When the door opened, Marilyn peeked out and asked, "Can you bring me my sleeping bag? It's in my bedroom closet. I'm going to sleep in Carolyn's room tonight."

Logan retrieved the sleeping bag and brought it back. "Do you want a night-light?" he asked as he walked out.

"The overhead light is fine," Carolyn said.

"And leave the door open," Marilyn added.

"Okay," Logan said. "Good night."

When he reached the kitchen, he pulled his

chair back from the table and sat down.

"What was that scraping noise?" Marilyn shouted.

"The chair," Logan answered.

He let out a yawn.

"That was you, right?" Carolyn called.

"Ye-es. Now go to sleep!"

Five minutes later, Logan heard footsteps and bumping. He went to the bottom of the stairs and listened.

The girls were whispering and moving things around.

Up went Logan again. "What's going on now?"

They were at the window, propping a Halloween mask between the shade and the glass.

"Just, you know, putting this here," Carolyn said.

"For protection?" Logan asked.

Marilyn scowled. "Just for decoration, that's all."

Logan nodded sagely and left.

Later he said he felt as if he'd been at a track workout, after all that stair-climbing.

He heard more noises but decided to stay put. When they finally settled down, about forty minutes later, Logan crept quietly upstairs.

The bedroom light was still glaring. Around Carolyn's bed and Marilyn's sleeping bag, standing shoulder-to-shoulder, were dolls, stuffed animals, and a model skeleton, in a big circle.

Guarding the twins. Keeping them safe.

Logan smiled. This time, when he went downstairs, he veered into the family room and flicked on the TV.

He sat on the sofa as the last part of *Horroville* flickered on the screen. In it, two girls were in a dark bedroom, clutching each other as footsteps approached.

Eeeeeee . . . Slowly a door opened. A silhouette appeared in the wedge of light that shone into the room.

The kids' mouths opened in an expression of horror.

"Go waaaaayyy!"

Logan nearly jumped to the ceiling. It was a real voice.

Carolyn's.

He ran to the stairs.

"Eh — " He choked on the word, then cleared his throat. "Everything all right?"

No answer. She must have been having a nightmare.

He ran back and turned off the show. Just in case they might have heard it through the ceiling.

Not that he was scared himself, you understand.

Not at all.

CHAPTER
6

WELCOME, HOME
LYNN

I put down my marker and examined the banner.

Then I double-checked the words in my dictionary. It was lying open to the *W* section on my desk, just below where I'd hung my handiwork.

I ran my index finger down to the word *welcome.*

Perfect.

Have I told you about my spelling? It's absolutely horrible. On the Claudia Kishi Dunce Meter, I believe it is the only topic below math. So I check everything.

I leafed through to the *H* section . . . *home.* No tricks there.

Lynn, I knew, was correct. I may not be a speller, but I do know my own middle name.

It was Saturday, about ten o'clock in the morning. In two hours, baby Lynn's life in the real world would begin.

Russ had already left for the hospital. At noon, he was going to bring Peaches and Lynn back to their house.

And when they arrived there — *Ta Da*!

Lynn's very first party. Courtesy of godmother Claudia and her family.

It had been a couple of days since Peaches had asked me the big question, but I was still flying. I had thought a lot about the responsibilities of being a godmother. I'd read that next to immediate family, the godmother should be the most important person in the baby's life. The job was not to be taken lightly.

At first I felt a little funny that Peaches hadn't asked Janine. I mean, Janine is Lynn's cousin, too. And she's the oldest in my generation.

I mentioned this to Janine, and she smiled. "You and Peaches have a special relationship. You deserve this, Claudia."

I thought that was nice of her. And I was determined to be the best godmother ever.

Starting with this wonderful, multicolored banner. I wanted it to be super-special. A keepsake. Someday, when Lynn was older, she would find the banner folded at the bottom of an old steamer trunk. Clutching it tearfully to her chest, she would remember her beloved godmother Claudia.

And remark on how perfect the spelling was.

"Janine, what do you think of this banner?" I called out my door.

Janine, who was still in pajamas and slippers, shuffled into my room. "Who's Home Lynn?"

"Huh?"

"Home Lynn," she repeated. "You wrote, 'Welcome, Home Lynn.' The comma is supposed to go after *Home*."

"Oh."

As Janine shuffled back, I did a slow burn. Then I reached in my supply drawer for a pair of scissors.

No, I did not go after Janine with them. (How dare you think that!) I carefully cut a circle around the comma. Then I put it where the comma belonged, traced around the circle, and cut *that* out.

I switched the two circles and taped them from the back. Then I crossed to the other side of the room to look.

Hideous. Lynn would cackle if she found this in the steamer trunk.

I had to set an example. No cutting corners for my goddaughter. I ripped down the banner and hung another swath of material. Back to the drawing board.

By the time my parents returned, Janine was dressed and my new banner was completed to perfection.

"Wagon train, ho!" my father called from downstairs.

I grabbed my camera off my closet shelf and slung it over my shoulder. Then I scoured my room for all the other presents I'd stashed away for Lynn, and I put them in a plastic bag. Last, I rolled up the banner, tucked it under my arm, and headed out to the car.

Dad opened the trunk. He pushed aside about a dozen bulging grocery bags.

"Your mother thought we ought to take them a lot of prepared food," Dad explained. "They'll be too busy to cook for a while, so they can eat some now and freeze the rest."

I told you my parents are smart.

With everything jammed into the trunk, we drove off.

At Peaches' house, we brought the bags into the kitchen. I set my camera down in the living room. Quickly Janine and I hung the banner over the front door, then went back inside to help. It took awhile to wedge all the food into Peaches' freezer, which was crowded with about a hundred half-empty pints of ice cream. (I helped by storing some of the ice cream in my stomach.) Then Janine and I dumped chips, salsa, pretzels, and M&Ms into separate bowls.

"*You* bought M&Ms?" I cried out in amazement.

"Peaches will be needing extra energy today!" Dad called back.

While Janine and I spread the appetizers around, Mom prepared a plate of cold cuts and Dad cleaned up around the house (which Russ had left a pigsty).

I set all my presents out in prominent places. The bright-colored wrapping paper really livened things up.

At eleven-forty-five we plopped onto the living room sofa.

Done. Whew. All we had to do was wait.

"Is your camera ready?" Janine asked.

I grabbed it and took the case off. "Ye — "

The readout on top of the shutter said zero.

"No film, right?" Janine said.

I sprang up. *"What am I going to do?"*

"It's all right," Mom said reassuringly. "Use your mind's eye."

"Those kinds of pictures don't go in albums!" I shot back. "Lynn will never know what she looked like on her first day home. Take me to the store!"

"But they'll be here any minute," Janine protested.

"I will not let my goddaughter down!"

Dad looked at his watch. *"Vámonos.* We'll hit the drugstore on Beech Street."

You have never seen two people move so fast. We hopped into the car and Dad tore off. I spent about five seconds in the drugstore and bought three rolls. Dad took off again as I loaded the camera in the front seat.

"Whoopee," Dad said. "We're a bit like Bonnie and Clyde."

As we turned onto Russ and Peaches' street,

guess whose car was driving along in front of ours?

"Oh, no!" I cried.

"Should I head them off at the pass?" Dad asked.

"Dad, this isn't funny. Can we make it there first if we go around the block?"

Honk-honk!

I could not believe it. My father was blowing his horn!

Russ waved to us in the rearview mirror. He blew his horn, too.

So much for our secret.

Oh, well. If you can't beat them . . .

I started taking pictures.

Baby Lynn's Trip Home from the Hospital in Dad's and Mom's Car, as Viewed from Behind.

Lynn's Dad's and Mom's Car, Stopped in the Driveway.

The Rear Door Being Opened by Lynn's Dad.

Baby Lynn Asleep in Her First Car Seat.

Peaches Cuddling Baby Lynn in Front of the House . . .

I was on the second roll before we walked inside.

Peaches' eyes moistened when she saw the banner. "Oh, my goodness, you didn't have to do that!"

I made Janine take a photo of me and Peaches and Lynn under the banner. Then I held Lynn closer, so she could see it firsthand.

She whimpered a little, then burped.

Well, Peaches and Russ adored our little *fiesta.* Janine put a classical music CD on the player and I danced around with Lynn.

She loved it. I could tell. She burped again, which was becoming her favorite mode of expression. Then, degassed and happy, she stared at me for a long time.

"So so seeeerious," I said as we twirled around.

Then, without warning, Lynn puked. Just a little white stuff out the side of her mouth, and it didn't seem to bother her a bit.

But Godmother Claudia was on the case. I took Lynn into the nursery that Peaches and Russ had set up. I lifted a cloth diaper from a stack and wiped Lynn's mouth.

Then I checked her own diaper, which was a little wet, so I changed it. She had a bit of a rash on her leg, so I put ointment on it.

"What a quiet, patient girl," I said.

She flailed her arm, whacking herself harmlessly in the head.

"You have a natural painter's stroke," I remarked. "Could you do that again?"

"Hey, don't hog the baby!" Russ called out.

"Come, your fans await," I whispered. Putting a cloth diaper on my shoulder for protection, I walked out to the admiring throng.

We all gabbed and laughed and ate and drank. I made sure Janine took practically a whole roll of pictures of Lynn and me.

Once in awhile, I let other people hold her. But most of the time I rocked her and looked into those deep, serious eyes.

When Peaches took Lynn into the nursery for a nap, I sank back against the couch cushions and sighed. "I already miss her."

Dad smiled. "Love at first sight."

"That's what I call major-league bonding," Russ remarked. "Way to go, Godmom."

A moment later I ducked into the nursery for a sneak peek. Peaches had wrapped Lynn up tight in a baby blanket, so that only her head showed.

From my baby-sitting experience, I recognized that method. It's supposed to remind newborns of that cozy *in utero* feeling.

"It's the baby burrito look," I said. "Very chic."

Peaches giggled. "Claudia, you've been so wonderful. Lynn is a lucky girl to have you in her life."

Peaches and I threw our arms around each other. We held each other, rocking silently, just enjoying the high, wispy sound of Lynn's breathing.

Eventually we headed back to the living room and joined the Kishi family gabfest.

About a half hour later, Mom stood up and said, "One thing I remember most about having a newborn: short visits were the best visits. So on that note . . . "

"No, don't be silly," Russ said.

"Stick around," Peaches insisted.

But Mom stood firm. She, Dad, and Janine hugged Peaches and Russ and said mushy good-byes.

"I'll stay," I volunteered. "To help out."

"Claudia . . . " Mom said.

"It's okay," Russ assured her. "I'll take her home later."

"Well, all right," Mom agreed. "But don't stay more than half an hour, Claudia."

I could tell why Mom had suggested that. Peaches did need some downtime. But I made myself useful. I cleaned up the kitchen and put the bowls in the dishwasher.

Then I watched Lynn sleep. And dreamed of all the stuff we were going to do together.

Russ invited me for dinner, and I accepted.

Peaches seemed pretty wiped out. She didn't say much at the table and excused herself early.

"Would you like me to stay over?" I asked Russ. "I could make some formula, do a nighttime feeding — "

"Thanks, Godmom," Russ said. "But not tonight. We'll take you up on it some other time."

It was seven-thirty when Russ drove me home. Mom was a little upset. She thought I'd stayed way too long. But she got over it. On a day like that, no one could remain in a bad mood.

As far as I was concerned, my stay hadn't been long enough.

I felt a slight nagging sensation as I went to sleep that night. A sort of Lynn withdrawal, I guess. But I didn't mind.

In eight more hours, I would see my goddaughter again.

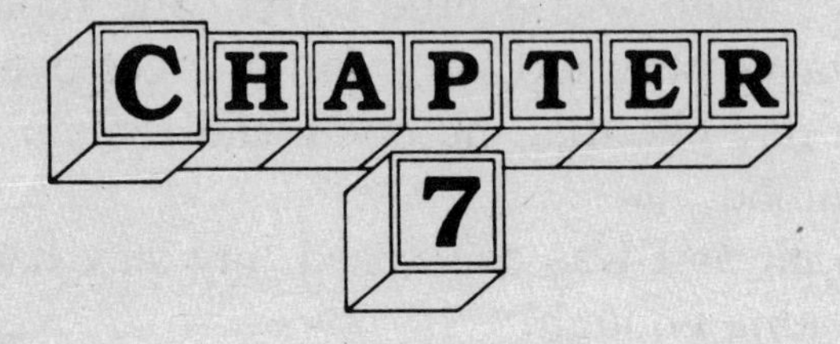

The Ghost of Russ answered the door Sunday morning. At least that was what he looked like. He was pale and hollow-eyed, his hair was all bunched up on one side, and he was wearing his pj's.

"Should I come back later?" I asked.

"Not if you agree to make coffee," he replied.

"Super Godmom to the rescue!" I said, walking past him to the kitchen. "Bad night, huh?"

"Night? Lynn thought it was daytime."

I laughed. "Newborns are like that. Their body rhythms are used to the darkness *in utero*."

"Ugh, it's too early for Latin," Russ said with a yawn.

I read the labels of the fresh-roasted coffees Dad had put in the freezer. "Breakfast blend okay?"

"Have caffeine, will drink."

I set the coffee bag by the electric-drip machine. "Okay, now how does this thing work?"

"Let me do it." That was Peaches, walking downstairs, her voice about five tones lower than usual. "Morning, Claudia."

"Morning!"

"*Eeeeeee!*" a teeny voice screamed from upstairs.

"I'll go," Russ volunteered, scampering to the stairs.

"No, I will."

The two of them disappeared, leaving me with the coffee machine.

How hard could it be? I lifted a hinged section in the back and poured in some ground coffee. Four . . . five . . . six tablespoonfuls. That seemed reasonable. I brought the machine to the sink, filled it with water, then set it back on the counter and pressed the on button.

Done. I ran up to see my goddaughter.

Peaches was sitting in a rocking chair, feeding Lynn. Russ was kneeling beside them, beaming.

What a picture.

"She looks bigger," I said softly.

Peaches laughed. "She should. She's been feeding all night."

"We have a real eater on our hands," Russ remarked.

(See? I knew we had a lot in common!)

"*Eeeeee!*" Lynn started up again.

Peaches lifted her onto a shoulder and started patting her back.

"Try a rubbing motion," said I, Claudia, the veteran of BSC-client newborns.

"Like this?" Peaches asked, moving her hand up and down Lynn's back.

"Here, I'll show you." I took Lynn and held her on my shoulder, moving my hand in a firm circular motion. "It stirs up the gas, but in a gentler way."

"*Eeeee!*" Lynn was not impressed.

I smiled. "Some babies are 'Eeee' babies. Others are more 'Aaaa.' Funny, I've never seen an 'Ohhhh' baby."

"*Brrrup,*" was Lynn's next contribution to the conversation.

"Atta girl," I said, handing her back to Peaches.

A faint sputtering noise filtered up from downstairs. "What's that?" Peaches asked.

"The coffee machine," I replied. "Don't forget to switch arms, Peaches. It's better for you and the baby."

Now I smelled something burning.

"Be right back," Russ said, hurrying out.

I followed him. "Don't go away," I called to Lynn over my shoulder.

In the kitchen, the coffee machine was coughing and spitting. A lumpy black liquid was gathering at the bottom of the pot.

"What did you do?" Russ asked.

When I explained, he immediately turned the machine off and pulled the plug. "Claudia, you put the coffee in the plastic basket above the pot. Only water goes in the back!"

I was mortified. "Sorry! Did I ruin it?"

"I don't know . . . "

"Is everything all right?" Peaches called from upstairs.

"Fine!" Russ lied.

"I'll clean it up!" I blurted out. "I'll buy you another one!"

After wiping up the guck and cleaning out the machine, I walked all the way to the deli and bought two cups of coffee (and a big Snickers bar to calm my nerves).

I devoted the rest of the day to making up for my goof. I did some shopping, gave Peaches dozens of tips, and changed lots of diapers.

Around noon Stacey and Mary Anne dropped by. Then Mallory and Jessi. Then Kristy and Abby. Of course I introduced them all to Lynn. You have never heard so many squeals of delight. Russ ended up serving us all lunch.

Peaches had only one nap the whole day. She and Russ were exhausted by dinnertime.

"Don't worry," I assured them. "You're in good hands."

I called home and told Mom I was going to stay and prepare dinner. Peaches and Russ kept insisting they didn't need me. They were being such troupers.

When I left at eight o'clock, they looked beat.

Lynn, however, was gurgling away.

I came that close to stealing her.

After such a Lynn-filled weekend, I could hardly bear the thought of going back to school on Monday.

I tried to pay attention in class. Really. But I had so many important things on my mind.

The whole week long I worked on three lists: Things to Make for Lynn, Things to Buy for Lynn, and Things to Do with Lynn.

Not that I was obsessed. I did learn a lot in social studies. Philadelphia, for example, is an extremely cool place. If it weren't for Philadelphia, the Constitution wouldn't have been written, Benjamin Franklin wouldn't have had a place to live, the country might have ended up pretty funky, my ancestors wouldn't have wanted to move here, and Lynn might not ever have been born.

I was psyched about our class trip. Not only because of the history, but also because we were going to stay over in a hotel. On Wednesday, Ms. Bernhardt passed out sign-up sheets for hotel roommates. We would be grouped two or three to a room.

"I'm going to request you," Melissa whispered.

I felt guilty. I'd written Abby's and Stacey's names on my list.

Underneath I wrote:

(Mellisa Banks, if the two grils are not avallable.)

That night I had another sitting job at the Prezziosos', so I could not see Lynn. I believe it was the hardest job of my career. When I put little Andrea to bed I almost burst into tears.

I made up for it after school the next day. I raced to Peaches and Russ's. I stayed an extra, extra long time. I taught Peaches how to double up the cloth diaper for longer use. I also gave her a few pointers on feeding technique.

Russ teased me about being so bossy. But

Peaches didn't seem to mind. She caught on well. She definitely had potential.

On Friday Ms. Bernhardt passed out the list of rooming assignments. I almost jumped out of my seat when I read it:

KISHI-STEVENSON-MCGILL.

"Rats," Melissa muttered.

"What's wrong?" I looked for Melissa's name and saw BANKS-KARP.

"Lily Karp," Melissa replied.

Frankly, I thought Melissa should be happy. I didn't know Lily that well, but she was smart and funny and friendly. She seemed like a perfect roommate.

"That's great," I remarked.

Melissa shrugged. "They didn't put you and me together. Want to trade?"

"Well, I —"

"I mean, like, Lily's cool and everything. She wouldn't mind. And, like — Stevenson and McGill? They're not in our class, so it's not even fair, and —"

"Stacey and Abby are two of my best friends, Melissa." Boy, was my Guilt Meter ticking. "But we're going shopping at the Washington Mall tomorrow. Want to come?"

Her face lit up. "Sure!"

The next day my dad drove Abby, Stacey, Melissa, and me to the Washington Mall. I found the world's most gorgeous canvas diaper bag for Peaches. Then I picked up a few necessities for the trip south: a pair of men's baggy summer-weight khaki pants, a sun dress, a few tank tops, sunglasses, and a Swiss army knife. (Why a knife? Don't ask me. Kristy said it was essential for a trip away from home.)

Melissa laughed at Abby's jokes, agreed with all our choices, and didn't say much else. Stacey was polite, but I could see she wasn't thrilled to have Melissa along. And I must admit, we couldn't totally be ourselves.

But hey, a good deed is a good deed, right?

The next few days passed in a blur. Because I was going to leave, I made sure to spend part of every day with Lynn. Each time I visited, I brought something new. Saturday night it was a coffeemaker (courtesy of my generous mom and dad). Sunday it was a pair of booties. Monday, three boxes of plastic diapers (for the nighttime; during the day Lynn wore cloth diapers).

Mom was becoming so cranky. She kept telling me to leave Peaches and Russ alone. "They need time together," she insisted.

Right. With a newborn in the house and absolutely no one to guide them? Puh-leeze.

The Tuesday before the trip, I spent the

whole afternoon at Peaches and Russ's. Things seemed okay until dinnertime. Peaches exploded when Russ dropped a plate. Then Russ exploded when one of Lynn's plastic diapers ripped. (Me? I kept my cool. Someone had to.)

After dinner Peaches said, "I'm turning in early."

"Fine," Russ snapped. "I'll stay up all night."

Peaches glared at him. "You don't have to say it that way."

"What way?"

"That was hostile, Russ. You know, I'm with her every day while you're at work. You don't know what that's like."

"Oh. And my life at work is so easy? What do you think I do at the office? Nap and play games?"

"What's that supposed to mean?"

"Nothing." Russ glanced sheepishly in my direction, then said to Peaches, "We really should discuss this another time."

But Peaches was steaming. "When? I never see you anymore!"

"That's because when we're alone, you're sleeping!"

"When else am I going to sleep? If I'm not running around with the baby, I'm entertaining. I feel like we're in a hotel here!"

"Well, that's not my fault!" Russ shot back.

I began inching toward the door. "Uh, guys? I think I'll just . . . head home."

"Sure, Claudia," Russ said. "Thanks for your help."

" 'Bye," Peaches said.

Out the door I went.

Whoa. I knew that having a child was a strain. I'd expected a little tension. But hearing a fight like that was a shock.

I felt bad for Peaches. She was losing it.

A hotel? The house sure didn't feel that way to me. Sure, my friends had visited that one day, but otherwise I'd seen hardly any other visitors. Evenings had been pretty cozy. Just Russ, Peaches, Lynn, and me.

Oh, well, they both needed sleep. That was the real problem. Maybe Lynn would cooperate that night.

One thing I was sure of. Peaches needed plenty of support.

I didn't know how they were going to survive the weekend without me.

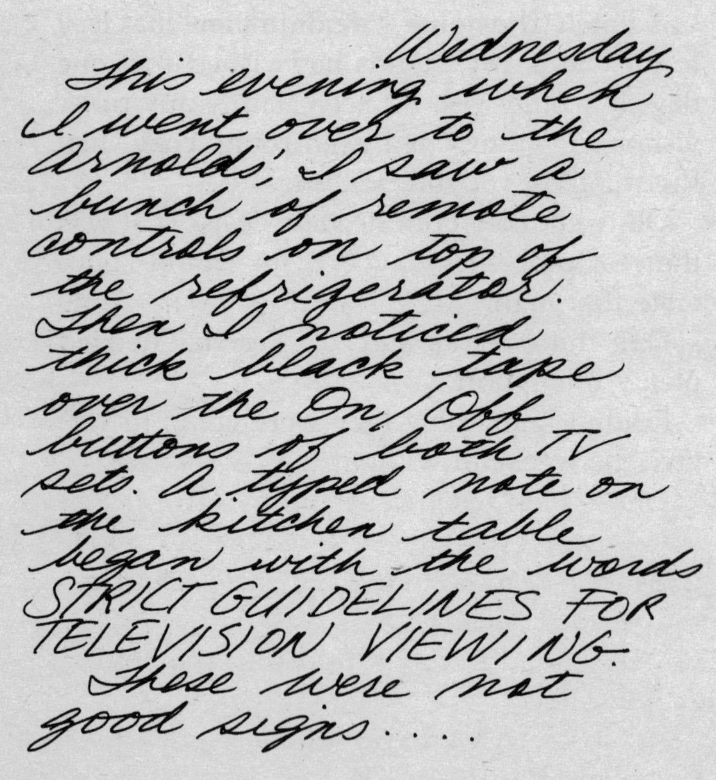

Wednesday

This evening when I went over to the Arnolds', I saw a bunch of remote controls on top of the refrigerator. Then I noticed thick black tape over the On/Off buttons of both TV sets. A typed note on the kitchen table began with the words STRICT GUIDELINES FOR TELEVISION VIEWING.

These were not good signs. . . .

"Carolyn," Mary Anne began patiently, "a human being cannot fit through an electrical outlet —"

"Can too!" Carolyn retorted. "It was in the movie!"

"You have to be affected by the liment of the planets and a field of magnets," Marilyn explained.

"I think you mean *alignment* of the planets," Carolyn corrected her. "And a magnetic field."

"Oh." Marilyn nodded.

"No!" Mary Anne said. "That's the explanation they used. But it's fiction. What you saw was fake."

"How do you know?" Marilyn asked. "You didn't see it."

"Well . . . I — I don't need to," Mary Anne sputtered. "I just know. They probably used trick photography."

"What about the chopped-off head, with all the blood?" Marilyn asked. "Was that real?"

Mary Anne felt herself turning green. "Of course not. It was rubber or plastic. The whole thing is just a movie! Look, guys, it's late. Time to put your pajamas on."

Marilyn and Carolyn tiptoed to the bottom of the stairs.

"RAAAAAAAAAAWWRRR!" they both bellowed upward.

"What are you doing?" Mary Anne asked.

"Sshhhh!" Carolyn said, cocking her ear.

"I think we scared it away," Marilyn whispered. "You go first, Mary Anne."

With a deep sigh, Mary Anne led the girls upstairs.

Marilyn's sleeping bag was still on Carolyn's floor. The electrical outlets were all taped up, and black-painted blocks had been stacked on the windowsill.

"What are those for?" Mary Anne asked.

"They'll fall to the floor if anyone tries to crawl in at night," Marilyn said, "so we'll know in advance. And we can run."

"We painted them black so they'll be invisible in the dark," Carolyn explained.

"Can you stand by the window while we change?" Marilyn asked.

As Mary Anne guarded the window, the girls grabbed their pajamas.

"Ready, set, go!" Marilyn said.

With a flurry of limbs, they practically tore their clothes off and leaped into the pj's.

Mary Anne laughed. "In a hurry to go to sleep?"

"Uh-uh," Marilyn said.

"We don't want to be *naked* if . . . you know," Carolyn added.

"If the monster comes?" Mary Anne asked.

The girls blushed.

Mary Anne accompanied them to the bathroom. She stood outside the door while they brushed their teeth. She let them roar into the hallway. She followed them back to their rooms.

Marilyn flicked on a desk lamp. The bedroom was as bright as Hermosa Beach at noon.

"Good night," Mary Anne said.

"Would you read to us?" Carolyn asked meekly.

"Okay," Mary Anne agreed. "What would you like to hear?"

"Where the Wild Things Are," Marilyn suggested.

Mary Anne is so sensitive. She did not tell them they were too old for picture books. She did not remind them they could read perfectly well on their own.

Instead she read the book to them. Then she read another request, *Harold and the Purple Crayon*.

Halfway through *There's a Nightmare in My Closet*, her eyes began to close. "Okay, you guys, sleeptime. Good night."

"Night," they mumbled.

Mary Anne went down to the kitchen. She glanced at the note on the table, which basically said that the twins' TV watching had to be strictly supervised. Then she took a copy of *The Catcher in the Rye* out of her backpack and settled down to read. (That, by the way, is one example of Great Literature I actually like.)

She enjoyed about three minutes of silence.

"Mary Anne, could you turn on the hallway light?" Marilyn suddenly called out.

"EEEEEEEEEEEEYYAHHHHHHHH!" Carolyn shrieked.

Mary Anne ran upstairs. Carolyn was huddled in her bed. A book lay on the floor by the door. "Take it away!" Carolyn cried.

"What's wrong?" Mary Anne asked.

"Scary pictures!" Carolyn blurted out.

Mary Anne scooped up the book, *Dr. Dredd's Wagon of Wonders*. It was lying open to a drawing of a dragon attacking a boy and girl.

"Mary Anne," Marilyn said timidly, "can we watch TV?"

Mary Anne let out a sigh. "Come on down."

Into the family room they went, after a detour to the kitchen, where Mary Anne retrieved the remotes.

"Do you still have free Boxoffice Busters?" Mary Anne asked as she pressed the On button.

Carolyn nodded.

"What channel is it?"

They both shrugged.

Mary Anne crossed her fingers and began to channel-surf.

Baseball . . . news . . . basketball . . . war movie . . . cooking show . . .

" . . . Last week we took you behind the scenes of an animation studio," a voice narrated over a montage of movie clips. "This week we go to the world of live action!"

"This looks good," Marilyn said.

Mary Anne sat back.

"Our feature tonight is, 'The Making of *Horrorville*'!"

Oh, groan. Mary Anne quickly pointed the remote.

"Leave it!" Carolyn cried.

"I can't," Mary Anne said. "Your parents don't want you to watch —"

A severed head leered out from the screen.

"AAAAAAAAAAUGH!" screamed the twins (and Mary Anne, too, I'll bet).

"So you see, the latex is coated with oil to give it a shiny texture," said a voice on the screen.

The camera zoomed back to show a balding guy in a cable-knit sweater. He cheerfully lifted the head up and admired it. "Horsehair is sewn into the scalp and matted down with a little shoe polish," he continued. "We created a mold for the mask's realistic features, using my assistant, Reginald."

Reginald entered the shot, grinning. He looked exactly like the head.

Marilyn and Carolyn were riveted.

"Many of the effects were the work of our computer animators." The man was now walking into a room where four people were clacking away on keyboards. "A two-second sequence, in which a man appears to ooze out of an electrical outlet, actually took a week to put together. First, we scanned the actor in a variety of positions and fed the coordinates into the program."

A grid appeared on the screen, showing the outline of an actor jumping slowly.

"The computer then compressed the limbs and added blurring to simulate fast motion . . . "

On the grid, the actor's outline squeezed at one end like a balloon. Next, the final version appeared: the "monster" who emerged from the outlet.

"That is sooooo cool!" Marilyn said.

Mary Anne put down the remote. It *was* cool. And the opposite of scary.

The narrator showed how an actor's eye was "built out" with makeup to make it look as if the eyeball were dangling. Then two scenes were shown — two children running in a field, and a flying vulture — and superimposed to create the illusion of a giant vulture chasing the kids.

For an hour, all the horrifying stuff was explained and demonstrated. Mannequins exploded, stuntpeople fell into big cushions, and plastic packets of fake blood were pinned onto actors' clothing and splattered by remote control sensors.

Mary Anne — the girl who covers her eyes during movie fistfights — wasn't grossed out one bit. She said the whole thing looked like a big game.

After the show, Marilyn and Carolyn were bouncing around the room, firing questions:

"Can we do that stuff on our computer?"

"How did Mary Poppins fly?"

"Did Old Yeller really die?"

"What about the Wicked Witch, when she melted?"

Mary Anne did the best she could. She knew about the witch dropping through a trap door. She also knew that the actor who played the Tin Man was a replacement because the first guy had a skin reaction to the silver paint.

"The wizard was a special-effects guy, too," Marilyn announced. "Dorothy was so dumb to think the big head was real."

"He had a computer behind the curtain," Carolyn said smugly.

Mary Anne just nodded.

After awhile, she fixed them a snack, made them brush their teeth again, and put them to bed.

Guess who went right to sleep that night? With only a night-light, too.

"Surprise!" I sang out.

As Peaches opened her front door, I held out a beautifully wrapped box. In it was the diaper bag I'd bought at the Washington Mall.

I'd brought it to school that morning in my bike basket, then stored it in my locker. That way I could go straight to Peaches' after school. It was Thursday, my last chance to see Lynn before my trip to Philadelphia on Friday. I needed maximum time.

"Oh, how sweet!" Peaches said. "A going-away present from the one who's going!"

"Open it," I said, stepping into the living room.

Peaches and I sat on the sofa. She eagerly ripped open the wrapping and lifted out the bag.

"It's adorable!"

I took it from her and unzipped it. "I know you already have one, but this one is more useful. It has three separate compartments, plus a removable changing pad. In here I put a bunch of stuff you'll need. For rashes, the zinc oxide works better than the ointment you have. Also, you'll want to switch to these contoured nipples, which will help Lynn's teeth grow straighter, even though they're latex, which wears out faster than plastic. I put in this soy-base formula, which you should try in case her fussiness is related to lactose-intolerance —"

"She's not lactose-intolerant," Peaches said.

"The way to tell is to switch for a few days and —"

"She's not lactose-intolerant," Peaches repeated. "I've been through this with the pediatrician, Claudia."

"Oh. Well, I can return it. Anyway, I found that the aloe baby wipes were irritating, but I'm not sure if it was because of the aloe or the scent, but you can throw them out anyway because I included some regular, unscented wipes."

"Thanks, Claudia. This is wonderful. Really —"

"And how is the cutest baby in the world?" I hopped up and headed for the nursery.

"Well, actually, she's —"

I opened the nursery door. Lynn was snoring away in the bassinet. As I walked in, my foot came down on a plastic rattle.

Crrrunch!

"EEEEEEEEEE!"

"Oh, my lord!" Peaches moaned. "She was sleeping!"

"Sorry," I said.

"I just put her down a minute ago. She was up at the crack of dawn and I didn't sleep last night, and —"

"I'll put her back to sleep." I lifted Lynn onto my shoulder. With each cry, her whole little body clenched up.

"Oh, so sad, so sad, little girl," I purred.

I could have said the same to Peaches. Her face was crumbling.

I bounced Lynn up and down and started to sing, "Wynken and Blynken and Nod one night . . . "

"EEEEEEEEEE!" screeched Lynn.

"That makes her worse, Claudia," Peaches said.

"What? The song?"

"No!" Peaches grabbed Lynn out of my hands. "The bouncing! You don't know *everything*!"

She spun away, carrying Lynn into the living room.

My mouth dropped so fast it almost hit the carpet.

She's stressed, I told myself. Post-partum depression was the technical term. I'd read about it. I'd seen clients go through it.

I was not going to take it personally. I marched into the living room with a smile on my face.

Peaches was changing Lynn's diaper on the sofa, using the diaper bag pad and a small diaper I'd packed.

"Turn the pad over," I suggested. "The other side is smoother."

Peaches did not respond. She did not turn the pad over, either. I could see her shoulders tense up.

"I'm just trying to help," I said.

Peaches sat on the sofa. Lynn was now quiet and dry and resting on her lap.

When Peaches spoke, it seemed as if she had to pry her teeth open. "I know you're trying to help, Claudia. And I didn't mean to snap at you, but —"

"I'm thinking of Lynn, that's all," I said.

"Well, yes, of course. But Lynn isn't the only one in this house, Claudia."

"I know *that*. That's why I've been cleaning up and cooking and doing stuff around the house. And telling you about all the techniques I've learned."

"And I'm grateful. Really. But I've picked up some techniques of my own, you know. Russ and I know Lynn pretty well, I think. We have a good routine now, with housework and shopping and cooking. We're pretty independent."

I was taking the hint. It felt like a sledgehammer over my head. "So you're saying you don't want me around anymore?"

"All I'm saying is this: if you want to know what I really need now, it's some quiet evening time with my little family."

"Right. And I'm nothing but a nuisance who breaks coffee machines and gives too much advice."

"Claudia, please —"

"Mom's been talking to you, hasn't she? I can tell. *She* made you think I was spending too much time here."

"That's silly," Peaches retorted. "Russ and I haven't talked to her at all about this."

"Oh, great. You decided I was a nuisance on your own. That makes me feel so special!" I grabbed my backpack and stomped toward the front door. "Well, you ought to be happy now. You won't see me for a whole weekend!"

"You're being unreasonable, Claudia —"

"At least *Lynn* appreciates me!"

WHACK! I let the screen door slam behind me.

"EEEEEEEEEE!" cried Lynn.

Boy, did I feel rotten.

That night Peaches called our house and asked for me. I refused to take the call.

Not because I was angry. I mean, I *was*, but that wasn't the main reason.

The main reason was clothes.

I had packed too many of them. My suitcase would not shut. At the moment Peaches called, I was sitting on my suitcase, trying to pull the zipper around. If I stood up right then, my entire wardrobe might have exploded all over the room.

"Rrrrrr . . . rrrrr . . . " I grunted.

This was ridiculous. Keeping my hand on the zipper, I bounced a few times. Each time I came down, I yanked.

That earned me another five inches or so. I was now more than halfway there. A huge bulge of clothing stuck out where the top and bottom didn't meet. It looked as if the suitcase were grinning at me in triumph.

I know. It was only one weekend. But think about it. It was May. Cold at night, warm during the day, good chance of rain. I brought a fuchsia cotton sweater for one night, a light cashmere one for the other, so I wouldn't repeat. I packed my summer-weight clothes, but they didn't go with either sweater, so I stuffed in a jeans jacket. Then a couple of heavier-weight outfits (in case of cold) and a nice dress (in case of fancy dinners), and appropriate footwear: sandals, sneakers, loafers, dress shoes.

The rain gear and boots, I think, were what really clogged things up.

Rrrrrring! went my phone.

I tensed. All my fury at Peaches welled up. I just knew she'd try me at this number.

I slid off my suitcase on the seventh ring. *Rrrrip*! went the zipper as it opened.

(Grrrrr.)

"Hello!" I barked.

"Are you taking a hat?"

"Who is this?"

"Melissa. I heard it's cold in Philadelphia."

"Well, it's *south*. If you don't wear one here, I don't think you'll —"

"I am soooo stupid." Melissa laughed hysterically. "Okay, see you!"

Click.

I couldn't believe it. For *that* dumb question, I had to lose the war of the zipper?

I returned to the Great Gaping Mouth. I dropped it on the floor and jumped on it.

Rrrrring!

"Hello?"

It was Melissa the Pest again. "I forgot to ask. Will there be toothpaste and soap and shampoo at the hotel?"

"I don't know," I replied.

"Hmm. I'll bring some. Thanks. Ooh, I'm so psyched!"

Click.

Duh.

I moved the phone right next to my suitcase, in case Melissa called to ask about toilet paper.

Then I went back to work.

If my suitcase hadn't had wheels, I think I'd be dead now. Mom drove me to school the next morning, but I alone had to take the suitcase to my social studies classroom.

It was like dragging a sleeping rhinoceros.

Ms. Bernhardt let us store our luggage for the day, so we could leave straight from school. I spent most of the day massaging my aching arms.

After the final bell, you could tell who were Ms. Bernhardt's students. They were stampeding down the hall.

Good old Abby helped me wheel the rhino outside.

"What's in here?" she asked.

"Just clothes," I replied.

Abby let out an exasperated sigh. "Claudia,

how many times did I *tell* you not to pack your suit of armor?"

Melissa came running up behind us. "Can I help?"

"We're fine," Abby said.

"No. Let me." She grabbed the strap, forcing Abby to step aside. Her foot clipped the side of the suitcase.

Thoomp! Down it went, sending up a cloud of dust.

"*Aaaa-choo!*" sneezed Abby the Allergic.

"Oops," said Melissa.

(Thank you, Melissa.)

Somehow, without renting a crane, we managed to load my suitcase onto the first of two buses marked with *Philadelphia* signs.

When I saw Stacey's two valises in the cargo area, wrapped with leather belts, I didn't feel so bad.

Stacey and I sat together, gabbing excitedly. Abby sat behind us, and Melissa plopped down next to her.

By the time Ms. Bernhardt gave instructions to both bus drivers and lectured us all on behavior, it was ten to four.

As we pulled away from SMS, everybody was singing, playing games, and chatting nonstop. The bus was huge and comfortable, with high-backed, soft seats. Which came in handy on the four-hour trip.

Especially after all my friends had dozed off.

As we trundled down the New Jersey Turnpike in the dusk, my mind was racing.

All I could think about was my argument with Peaches.

Pest. Claudia the Pest.

I could just imagine Lynn at age six or so, looking out the window as cousin Claudia drives up to visit. Is she excited to see me? Noooo, because Peaches has told her what a pest I am.

Maybe Russ and Peaches chose the wrong person to be Lynn's godmother. Maybe they should have asked Janine. Perfect people aren't pests.

I stared out the window. Rain was beading on the pane, then dripping slowly downward.

Or maybe it was the reflection of my tears. It was hard to tell.

"We are now passing under the Benjamin Franklin bridge," the bus driver announced. "To your left is the Delaware River — and directly in front of us is Philadelphia, Pennsylvania!"

My face was plastered to the window. So was Stacey's. Two little breath-circles were forming on the glass.

Outside we could see the lights of the Philadelphia skyline. Along the river, boats chugged slowly.

Now Ms. Bernhardt had the bus driver's mike. "We are approaching Penn's Landing. This is where the young Benjamin Franklin came ashore from Boston, penniless and homeless. He would one day become the definer and tamer of lightning, the founder of the first lending library, the first postmaster general . . . "

As I was about to doze off, the bus turned,

and Ms. Bernhardt pointed out the Liberty Bell a block away (I couldn't see it) and Independence National Park (I was busy checking out a mall called the Bourse).

We pulled to a stop near a big luxury hotel that overlooked the park. A brightly lit sign advertised a health club, pool, sauna, twenty-four-hour room service, award-winning restaurant, and nightly entertainment.

My heart leaped. I squeezed Stacey's hand.

When the light turned green, the bus kept driving.

Sigh.

Parts of Philadelphia were pretty cool. Out the window I spotted a little cobblestoned alleyway, no wider than a horse and cart. Brick houses faced each other on either side, so close you could open your window and have a quiet chat with your across-the-street neighbor.

I felt a little shiver. I expected a girl in an eighteenth-century dress to come out one of the front doors with a butter churn.

The next moment — *whoosh* — the wrinkle in time had disappeared. We were on a street that reminded me of present-day New York City.

The bus pulled up to a six-story brick building next to a small diner. "Last stop, the Pepperidge Inn!" the bus driver called out.

"I call the Jacuzzi first!" Stacey said.

Abby was groggy and achy from her nap. "I need some time in the pool."

"Let me at the refrigerator," I added.

We piled out of the bus. The hotel's electric doors whisked open and a team of concierges charged out. They took all our luggage, while we retired to our luxury suites overlooking the river.

I wish. (Fooled you, huh?)

We had to drag our own luggage through the front doors. The art on the walls was atrocious and the carpet clashed with the lobby's color scheme. We were greeted by a gray-haired man eating a ham sandwich at the front desk.

"You the Stoneybrook contingent?" he asked.

When Ms. Bernhardt said yes, the man slapped a little bell. A sleepy guy in a polyester uniform appeared from around the corner and scooted behind the desk to pull keys from a pegboard.

Okay, so the Pepperidge Inn was not exactly the Plaza. But you know what? None of us cared. We were chattering away happily. I don't know what it is about overnight class trips. I guess being away from home makes everything exciting.

A moment later, Ms. Bernhardt shushed us and began calling out room numbers. Abby,

Stacey, and I were on the second floor, Room 204. Melissa and Lily were in Room 217.

"Can't we be in, like, two-oh-six?" Melissa cried. "Ms. Bernhardt, can we switch into the room next to Claudia?"

I cringed. Abby rolled her eyes. Lily looked embarrassed.

"Melissa, *please,*" Mrs. Bernhardt hissed. Then she turned to the crowd and announced, "Listen up. A parent chaperone will be staying on each floor. Make sure you know what room he or she is in. In fifteen minutes, at exactly eight o'clock, we'll gather in a large meeting room, where a buffet supper is being set up. So get cracking!"

Our chaperone was Lily's mom. She helped us lug our suitcases onto the elevator. We rode up to the second floor and found our room.

I pushed the door open and turned on the light.

How was our room? Well, fabulous, if you like industrial carpeting and worn-out olive-green bedspreads and TVs that are chained to the wall.

Abby darted into the bathroom. "Ugh, no Jacuzzi."

"Jacuzzi?" Stacey cracked up. "How about running water?"

Psssshht! went the tap. "Yup! We're in luck!"

Abby walked out, smiling. "I love old, funky places."

"Didn't Ms. Bernhardt say it was a historic hotel?" I asked.

"I think Ben Franklin was the last guest," Stacey remarked.

Honestly, it wasn't that bad. We were just in a goofy mood.

I unzipped my suitcase. The top sprang open and hit the wall with a thud. My clothing, grateful to be free, bounced up as if it were alive.

"Aaaugh!" Abby shrieked. "The wardrobe that ate Philadelphia!"

"Hurry and claim some drawer space," Stacey warned her, "or you'll be sorry."

The mad dash was on. We yanked clothes out of our suitcases and stuffed them in the drawers. Shirts, pants, jackets, bras, hair driers, it didn't matter. In they went.

In two seconds we were on the floor, howling with laughter.

In mid-howl, I turned to see Melissa staring at us. "Hi. Uh, your door was open."

"HOOOOOO-HA-HA-HA!" Why did that statement seem so funny? I have no idea.

Melissa started laughing, too, for no reason. Somehow, that made us laugh even more.

I don't know how we made it to the meeting

room in time, but we did. With Melissa right behind us, totally ignoring Lily.

I raced to the buffet table. Unfortunately, Alan Gray threw a body block and grabbed a plate before me. "Oops! Squeeze me," he said with his typical goony laugh.

What a dork.

I made sure to avoid anything his hand brushed against. I sampled all the regional cuisine, including an exquisite cheesesteak hoagie (which was really a big roast beef sub with onions and cheese), but I avoided something labeled Phamous Philly turtle soup. (The thought was revolting.)

Abby, Stacey, and I found four seats together at the end of the table. We sat in three of them.

Melissa, who was looking for a table with Lily and her mom, ran over to us and took the fourth seat.

"Meliss*aaaa*," Lily complained.

"Sorry, Lily, not enough room." Melissa grinned at me, then pointed at a roll on Stacey's plate. "Do you want that?"

"Melissa, you were just on line!" Stacey reminded her.

"I thought we could only take one," Melissa replied. "I love rolls. Just like Claudia. Right, Claud?"

I didn't respond. I was too busy shoveling.

Melissa picked up her hoagie. "So, I guess this is our table for the weekend, huh?"

Puh-leeze.

Fortunately, Ms. Bernhardt stood up to speak. "Listen up, brave travelers! Here's our schedule in brief: Tonight we stay in the hotel. Tomorrow we meet here for breakfast at seven-thirty, then take a historical tour of Independence National Park, maybe visit Betsy Ross's house and the U.S. Mint —"

"I *love* mint," I whispered to Abby. Boy, was I ready for dessert.

"Then lunch at the Gallery," Ms. Bernhardt went on, "where you can do some shopping if you like." (Now she was talking!)

"We're going to shop until we drop, huh, Claud?" Melissa said.

We? Oh, groan . . .

"After that," Ms. Bernhardt continued, "we'll board the buses again and hit the museums, then have an early dinner and — here's my big surprise — we're going to the theater!"

"All riiight!" Abby cried.

Overall, a pretty cool schedule. I couldn't wait.

My dessert selections for the evening, should you be interested, were cheesecake, ice cream, and something called shoofly pie (which was brown and sweet and made with molasses). On the way back to our room, Stacey, Abby, and I stopped off at the snack and soda machines near the laundry area.

With chips, pretzels, and chocolates, we went upstairs and had a symposium about the Declaration of Independence.

Well, actually, we watched the hotel's movie channel and ate and laughed.

The trip was off to a fabulous start.

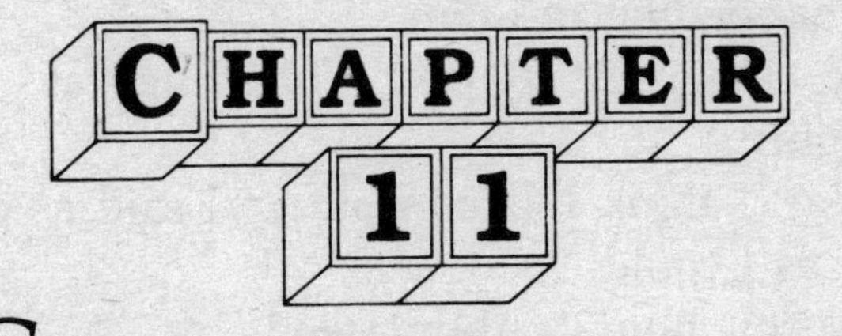

"Claudia, are you okay?"

My eyes opened. Stacey was in her pj's, sitting at the edge of her twin bed. Abby, who had slept on a roll-away cot, was looking at me curiously.

An awful dream was slowly fading from my mind. "Fine," I replied. "Just a nightmare."

"You were moaning," Stacey said.

"A visit from the ghost of Benny Franklin?" Abby asked.

I tried to hold on to the image. "Baby Lynn was running through a big field, on those teeny legs. She was heading toward a cliff. I was running and running, trying to catch her."

"Sounds like Holden Caulfield," Stacey said. "You know, that scene in *The Catcher in the Rye,* where he imagines himself catching all the kids near the cliff?"

That was it. Mary Anne had mentioned

reading that book at the Arnolds'. I must have been thinking of it.

Whew. For a minute I'd been afraid that the dream was a premonition. That something bad was happening to Lynn.

My stomach started fluttering at the thought.

"Um, I think I'll call home," I said as casually as I could.

"At this hour?" Abby asked.

Ehhhhhhhhhhhh!

The clock radio alarm gave me a jolt. We'd set it for seven o'clock, which gave us half an hour until breakfast.

"Last one to the privy is a colonial guttersnipe!" Abby called out in a fake British accent.

(I don't know where she comes up with this stuff. She must have a writer.) Stacey and I scrambled into the bathroom after her.

We brushed. We washed. We combed. We elbowed each other. We ran back out to change.

Somehow we managed to emerge from our room looking halfway human. Then we barreled down the hall to the elevator.

"Wait for me, guys!" Melissa's voice called out.

A couple of businessmen in the elevator were not happy to be waiting for Melissa. (Frankly, I wasn't thrilled about it, either.)

We rode down and showed up at breakfast on time.

The first thing I noticed at the buffet table was Eggs Benedict. The next thing I noticed was a dish of canned peaches among the condiments.

Peaches. Benedict. Coincidence or omen? You be the judge.

Thinking about Peaches made me think of Lynn. I had a huge pang of longing. I wanted to call just to hear Lynn's breathing on the phone. I missed her so much. Did she miss me? Was her diaper rash improving?

Was I being ridiculous or what?

I chose Belgian waffles, scrambled eggs, bacon, and a small bowl of Frosted Flakes. (Shopping in an unfamiliar mall, I was going to need extra energy.)

Melissa, of course, sat next to us. As we stuffed our faces, Ms. Bernhardt handed out a list of groups. Eight kids were assigned to each parent/teacher chaperone. Ours was Mrs. Karp. Melissa was in the group.

Melissa nudged me. "I pulled strings," she said with a grin.

(Lucky us.)

"Okay, before we leave, this word from your sponsor," Ms. Bernhardt announced. "We'll be doing a lot of walking in some crowded places, and the groups may split up from time to time. So remember rule number one: You are to stay with your group at all times. No straggling, no haggling. Your parent/teacher chaperone is boss . . . "

Blah, blah, blah. My eyes wandered back to the buffet table. The workers were clearing the Belgian waffles, and I was dying to have just one more.

Abby elbowed me and I snapped back to attention.

" . . . the address of the hotel. Remember, this is not just a historical site but a major city. Be careful, have fun, stick together, and remember, you are representatives of Stoneybrook, and anything you do reflects on you, your friends, and your town. Now let's finish up and go!"

I dug into the rest of my breakfast.

"Representatives of Stoneybrook?" Abby murmured.

"Puh-leeze," I said, "as if total strangers will know where we come from, just by looking at us."

Melissa giggled. "It's like, oh wow, those girls are so bad? So let's, like, ask where they came from so we can, you know, never go to their horrible town?"

Uh-huh. Right.

Abby smiled politely. Stacey cleared her plate.

Fortunately my mouth was full and I could not respond.

A few minutes later we were outside, walking the sidewalks of Philadelphia. It was gorgeous and clear, and my jeans jacket was the perfect weight.

We detoured through the alleyway I had seen on the bus ride. Alan Gray decided to test the echo by neighing like a horse. (Would this occur to anyone but Alan? I doubt it.)

At Independence Park, we saw a great historical film in the visitors' center and then went on a guided walking tour. I actually choked up when I saw the crack in the Liberty Bell. I could picture the joyous, tear-streaked face of the young colonist who caused that crack by ringing in the news of independence with so much enthusiasm. (The guide told us that was just a legend, but I believe it anyway.)

We saw the hall where the Declaration of Independence was adopted, and the house where Thomas Jefferson drafted it. We threw pennies on Ben Franklin's grave. We sat in the pews of the church Franklin and George Washington went to. We checked out Betsy Ross's house.

By lunchtime, I was beat. But I perked up after we trudged over to the Gallery. (Malls do that to me.) We ate at a fabulous bagel restaurant, and Mrs. Karp gave us half an hour to browse.

She and Lily disappeared into a record store. Abby went with them to find a present for Anna. Stacey and I went boutique-hopping. I bought some hoop earrings for me and a few souvenirs for the rest of my family. For Lynn I picked up an adorable little dress, a pair of pj's, some bath toys, and a Philadelphia t-shirt. Melissa tagged along, begging us to go to look at some new CDs. (Why she hadn't gone with Lily, I don't know.)

"Ugh, I'm broke." Stacey groaned as we walked out to the bus, which was waiting at the curb.

"I'll float you the rest of the day," I said, checking my pockets. "I have two dollars and eleven cents."

"Thanks a lot," Stacey said as we climbed aboard.

Soon we were trundling along a tree-lined boulevard toward the Philadelphia Museum of Art. Mrs. Karp turned from her seat in front of us and said, "We have until four o'clock. The bus is going to stop at three places: the art museum, the Franklin Institute Science Museum, and the Academy of Natural Sciences Museum. Let's choose one, and if we have time, we can walk to the others."

"What about the Rodin Museum?" I asked.

"Who's Row Dan?" Melissa asked. (Shades of Kristy Thomas.)

"*Rodin,*" Lily told her. "It's French. He was a great sculptor."

(Sigh. If someone had to attach herself to us, why couldn't it have been Lily?)

"We can go if there's enough time and interest," Mrs. Karp said.

We decided on the Philadelphia Museum of Art. Abby made us all climb the endless steps while she sang the *Rocky* theme. (Could we have taken the convenient street-level entrance? Noooo.)

I always forget how time speeds up in an art museum. At least for me it does. I become hypnotized by great paintings. I can stand in front of one and see a million different things in the light and texture and perspective and composition — and when I look up, twenty minutes have passed.

Unfortunately, I am not terrific company for non-artistic types. After a couple of rooms, Abby and Stacey scooted ahead of me.

Melissa did not. At first I assumed she loved art, too. But she kept making these dumb comments, such as "I did something like that in kindergarten," or "That would look nice in my den."

Finally I heard her say, "It's almost three-thirty. Can we go now?"

Enough. I spun around angrily. "*You* can go whenever — wait a minute. Three-thirty? Are you sure?"

"Uh-huh."

I slumped on a wooden bench. "Oh, groan. I wanted to see the Rodin Museum."

"Where is it?" Melissa asked.

"We passed it on the way — the one with the statue in front, about four blocks away?"

"That's close. Let's go."

"No way, Melissa! We can't just leave. Remember what Ms. Bernhardt said —"

"Oh, come on! We'll just, like, run there and look, then run back! Who'll know?"

It was definitely tempting. "Well . . . I guess we could ask Mrs. Karp."

"We'll never find her. Let's just do it."

"I don't know. The bus leaves in half an hour . . . "

"You've been to New York City, right?" Melissa said. "There, a block takes one minute to walk. So if Philly's the same, that's an eight-minute round trip. That gives us twenty minutes to look at sculptures!"

Melissa sounded so confident. And twenty minutes would be better than nothing.

What the heck. Who knew if I'd ever have this chance again? "Let's do it," I said.

We ran outside and headed back down Benjamin Franklin Parkway.

Melissa had just enough money for two admissions. When she saw the statue *The Thinker*, she remarked, "What a hunk."

I gave her a Look.

"Of marble, I mean," she quickly added.

If you have never checked out Rodin sculptures, you must. They are so fluid and voluptuous, you can't believe they're made of stone.

I wish time were, too. Fluid and voluptuous, that is.

It's neither. When I looked at my watch, it was eleven after four.

"Oh my lord!" I exclaimed. "Melissa, we're late!"

We raced to the door. We took a left and bolted.

After a couple of blocks, absolutely nothing looked familiar. "This isn't the right way," I said.

I started to run back, but Melissa grabbed my arm.

"Claudia, the street to the museum runs *diagonally*, right? If we go up this side street, we'll cut off the triangle and save time."

"Huh?" Geometry. I could feel my eyes glaze.

"I saw it on a map. Come on."

We ran and ran, peeking up and down each cross street for a familiar landmark.

Finally we stopped. Melissa was out of

breath, looking around frantically. A half block away I spotted a subway station, near a hospital. "Race-Vine Station," I read. "Is that near the museum?"

Melissa shrugged. "How should I know?"

We sprinted to the subway stop. The fare was posted in bold numbers. A dollar fifty each.

I reached in for my two dollars and eleven cents.

"How much money do you have?" I asked.

"Nothing. I spent it at the museum."

I was seeing red. "Great, Melissa, just great. We're lost. And it's your fault."

"*My* fault? *You* wanted to go, didn't you?"

"Excuse me? I was the one who said we didn't have time. But no. *You* said we did."

"Well, I was just trying to help —"

"And who led us here? I thought we were going to cut off the triangle, Melissa! Now where are we? Ms. Bernhardt's probably having a heart attack. Maybe if we just lie here on the sidewalk and make *X*'s with our bodies, the search helicopters will find us in a few hours."

Melissa's lips quivered. "We could call."

"I don't have a quarter. Do you?"

Melissa shook her head.

"Honestly, Melissa, you are the world's biggest pest!"

The dam suddenly burst. Melissa started crying.

Wonderful. Just wonderful. I was totally lost and broke in the middle of a strange city.

Just like the young Ben Franklin.

Worse. He didn't have to deal with a blubbering thirteen-year-old girl he didn't like. And two social studies classes who probably thought he'd been kidnapped.

I was in deep, deep trouble.

Saturday

Step aside, Mr. Spielberg! Watch out, Warner Brothers! We're dissing Disney!

That's right, folks! You are hereby invited to the world premiere of the Thomas-Arnold Film Festival!

Kristy

I'm glad somebody was having fun on Saturday. While I was stewing and Melissa was watering the sidewalks of Philly with her tears, Kristy was baby-sitting for the Arnold twins.

And listening to a blow-by-blow description of "The Making of *Horrorville*."

"You know that dangling eye?" Carolyn said eagerly, pacing across the family room floor. "It's just rubber. They attach it with makeup."

Kristy pretended to be shocked. "Really?"

"Yup," Carolyn replied. "And the actor doesn't even feel it. The people who play all those gross monsters are normal like us. When they're not filming, they just walk around with their plastic guts hanging out, like, 'La la la, hi, how's it going? What's for lunch?' "

"And you know what else?" Marilyn continued. "The ghosts who come through the window, and the guy who squeezes out of the electrical socket? Not real. They're both computer grappics."

"Gra*phics*, dummy," Carolyn said.

Marilyn stuck out her tongue. "You're the dummy!"

Kristy flipped into Damage Control Mode. "Whoa, hold it. I want to hear more about those special effects."

"Why?" Marilyn asked. "Are you scared, too?"

"Well, no. I mean, I don't watch too many of these movies, but —"

"You should," Carolyn said. "I want to be a horror movie director when I grow up. It's so cool."

"Me, too," Marilyn added.

Zing! Zap! Boiiiing!

Kristy's idea mill was cranking up. She spotted three shrink-wrapped, blank video cassettes on the den shelf. "Do your parents have a camcorder?"

Carolyn's face lit up. "Yes!"

"We can make a movie!" Marilyn exclaimed.

"Great idea!" Kristy said. "I mean, if your parents will allow it."

"They will!" Carolyn said. "As long as we're supervised and we use a blank tape."

"We have plenty of those," Marilyn added.

"Let's see, we could call it *Twin Terror,*" Kristy mused, "Or *Horror at the Arnolds'* . . ."

"I know!" Carolyn blurted out. "*The Twin Who Mutilated Her Sister.*"

"I'm the one who mutilates!" Marilyn called out.

"No way!"

"Way!"

"How about," Kristy interrupted, "*The Twins Who Mutilated Their Baby-sitter*?"

"YEAAAAHHHH!"

"Okay, what's our plot?" Kristy asked.

"Um . . . Carolyn and I play twins," Marilyn declared.

"Good start," Kristy said.

"Our baby-sitter is mean," Carolyn went on.

"And ugly," Marilyn added.

"Thanks a lot," Kristy harrumphed.

"Not in real life. It's a movie, silly!" said Metro-Goldwyn-Marilyn.

"One day our baby-sitter comes over," Carolyn continued, "and she's so disgusting we plot to destroy her."

"By mutilating her!" Marilyn squealed, as if she were suggesting a really fun sleepover.

"And we develop all these superpowers, so she can't escape," Carolyn concluded.

"I like it," Kristy said. "I see a future in directing for you both. Now, find me the camera. I'll load it while you guys figure out the makeup and props. We'll use the kitchen table as our base of production."

Marilyn ran to the den closet and fished out the camcorder. As Kristy loaded it, the twins scampered upstairs.

Every few minutes Kristy would hear a gale of laughter, and the twins would run down with something else. Before long the table was full of junk.

"What are the cotton balls for?" Kristy asked.

"We'll draw an eyeball on one," Marilyn explained. "Then you can squeeze it under your eyebrow and it'll look like your eye."

"And then, when it falls out — ew! Ew! Ew!" Carolyn screamed.

Marilyn pointed to a tan-colored piece of Play-Doh. "We'll plaster that over your ear and cover it with ketchup, for the part where you tear your own ear off."

"In frustration," Carolyn added.

Kristy picked up an aging hunk of olive-green Play-Doh flecked with red. "What's this for?"

Marilyn and Carolyn looked at each other. Then they cracked up so hard they could barely speak.

"Boogers," Carolyn finally managed to say.

"For your nose," Marilyn elaborated.

The fright wig was self-explanatory. As was the ripped Oxford shirt from the rag pile.

Kristy's costume.

Charming. (I told you Kristy was dedicated.)

Taking a deep breath, Kristy grabbed the camera. "Ready to start?"

"No, no, no!" Carolyn declared. "We must rehearse. Now Kristy, you go to the door and ring the bell . . . "

Kristy obeyed. The twins answered the

door, looking all smiley and innocent. "Hi, there, Kristy, so nice to see you!" Marilyn began. "Now, you growl and say, like, 'What's so nice about it?' "

"Do we have to use my real name?" Kristy asked.

Marilyn put her hands on her hips. "Who's the director, us or you?"

Kristy wanted to crack up. She didn't mind taking orders at all. She is such a ham.

The rehearsal was pretty basic. The two directors became more and more creative after the filming started. They made Kristy play a total jerk, yelling at them and eating all their food and not letting them watch TV and tying them to kitchen chairs.

Then Kristy filmed the twins soaking up rays from a distant star (a fluorescent sticker in the bathroom). Next they developed superpowers, burst out of their ropes, and flexed their muscles.

They filmed Kristy picking her nose in the living room, as she pretended to eat an old pair of Marilyn's sneakers.

Then Kristy held the camera upside-down, so it looked as if the twins were sneaking up to Kristy by walking on the ceiling.

The attack was spectacular. Kristy's ear-tearing scene was Oscar-caliber. And the fright-wig/ripped-shirt/boogers-and-ketchup getup? Too glamorous for words.

Really, you had to see this. We did. We have never laughed so hard in our lives.

You'll be happy to know the twins no longer have a bit of trouble going to sleep at night. But they do pester their parents all the time about seeing gory horror movies.

As for Kristy, she made a copy of the video for herself.

She's thinking of submitting it to a film festival.

"Yo, it's Claudia Kishi, the star of *Home Alone Thirteen: Lost in Philadelphia!*"

Alan Gray cracked up at his own stupid joke.

So did his pals Pete Black and Justin Forbes, and about five or six other kids who passed by my table. Just about everyone else ignored me.

It was Saturday evening. Ms. Bernhardt had reserved a room for all of us at a restaurant called Le Harborside. It's supposed to be a seafood restaurant, but as far as I was concerned, I might as well have been in the Sing-Sing mess hall. My appetite was gone, and my classmates were looking at me as if I were an ax murderer.

If they were looking at me at all.

Melissa was sitting at the opposite end of the restaurant with Lily and her mom. All three of them were staring glumly at their bread plates.

To be honest, I was surprised that my roommates agreed to sit with me. I didn't think they'd want to risk being in the path of flying steak knives.

Yes, Melissa and I had survived the afternoon. Barely.

Standing on the sidewalk near the subway station, Melissa started wailing. A gray-haired guy in a suit passed by and gave her a concerned look. "Is everything okay?" he asked.

Great. Now we were being accosted by strangers. "Fine," I replied. "We just can't find the art museum, that's all."

"Cheer up." He smiled and pointed down the street. "It's two blocks that way."

"Really? Thanks!" I said.

Melissa and I sprinted.

The place we reached was a much smaller building than the Philadelphia Museum of Art. No *Rocky* steps, no tree-lined parkway approach. A sign outside said *The Museum of American Art of the Pennsylvania Academy of the Fine Arts.*

Any other time, I would have been thrilled. I found out later it was America's first art museum.

But Melissa and I only went as far as the information desk.

"Excuse me," I said to the clerk. "But do you know where the Pepperidge Inn is?" (I figured that by now Ms. Bernhardt must have called the hotel asking about us.)

The clerk shook her head and reached under her desk. "Not offhand, but I do have a map and a phone book."

"Uh, the problem is, we're kind of —"

"Lost," Melissa blurted out.

The clerk's eyes widened. "You aren't the girls from Connecticut, are you?"

"How did you know?" I asked.

"We had a call about you, from your teacher. She was checking local art museums, because one of you is an artist or something?"

"That's me," I said, feeling for a teeny moment like a celebrity.

"Mr. Douglas, I found them!" the woman shouted across the floor. *"The lost girls from Connecticut!"*

A balding man came jogging toward us with a big smile. "Thank goodness!"

A round of applause broke out. Museum-goers were staring at us, clapping.

Forget about celebrityhood. I felt like a total goon.

"Come into the office," Mr. Douglas said. "Your teacher left a number. You can use our phone."

"Pepperidge Inn," a voice greeted me.

"Hi, it's Claudia! I mean, Kishi. And Melissa Banks. The lost girls from Connecticut?"

"Hold, please."

My knuckles were white from gripping the phone so hard. I was on the verge of total hysteria, and the phone was playing the "Doe, a Deer" song in my ears.

Right after "Fa, a long, long way to run," Ms. Bernhardt's voice cut in: "Hello, Claudia?"

At least I assumed it was her voice. I have never heard it so tense and frightened and angry.

"H-hi," I said, choking back a sob.

"Are you all right? Where are you? Is Melissa with you?"

I nodded. (Real smart.) "Y-yes. We're — " *Sniff*. "At, at —"

I looked at the clerk. She whispered the museum's long name and I repeated it.

"Stay there, I'm coming in a cab to get you. I don't want you two traveling alone another minute."

"I'll pay for it," I volunteered. "Will two dollars and eleven cents be enough?"

I don't need to tell you what the answer to that was. Ms. Bernhardt arrived in the cab about ten minutes later. She did not seem terribly happy.

In fact, she lectured us all the way back to the hotel.

Okay, it was more than a lecture. It was somewhere between a shriek and a bellow. "I had just called the police!" she cried. "Then I had to call them back to say 'Never mind.' Do you think they appreciated that? Don't you think they had better things to do than chase after two wayward thirteen-year-olds? And did you stop to think about your classmates? A whole busload of them is sitting at the hotel, waiting. Poor Mrs. Karp feels horrible. She's blaming herself for your inconsiderate, selfish behavior!"

"Sorry," I said.

Melissa and I must have repeated that word a thousand times during the trip. Ms. Bernhardt did soften up a bit toward the end. She admitted she was happy to see us, and she told about a time she wandered away from her parents at the Grand Ole Opry when she was a girl.

When we reached the Pepperidge Inn, the bus was parked in front and our classmates were clogging the sidewalks and the lobby. Staring at us.

From their expressions, I half-expected to find twin electric chairs awaiting us by the front desk.

I was glad Ms. Bernhardt allowed us to go to the restaurant. I guess she couldn't have iron bars and a lock installed in our hotel room windows in time.

"I think I'm going to have a New York steak," Abby said, perusing the menu.

"Abby, this is *Philadelphia*," Stacey reminded her.

"I don't see pretzels with mustard listed here," Abby replied.

"Well, I'm having snapper soup and soft-shell crabs," Stacey declared. "How about you, Claudia?"

"Try some fish," Alan the eavesdropper called out. (He was at the next table. Lucky me.) "They never stray from their school!"

This time the whole room seemed to burst into laughter. I sank in my seat. I wanted to run to the dock and ride off on a motor boat.

Somehow I made it through dinner, but I didn't eat much. I was thrilled to go to the theater afterward. Being in a dark place where no one could see me or talk to me was just perfect.

The show was great, too, and really appropriate — a revival of the musical *1776* at the Forrest Theater. After having studied all the important stuff Jefferson, Franklin, and Adams did, it was nice to see they could sing and dance, too.

Abby, of course, did her own renditions in the room later on. How was she? Well, let's just say the talent scouts were not breaking down the doors of the Pepperidge Inn that night.

Stacey and Abby both wanted to hear all the details of my horrible afternoon. Somehow, as I was telling it, the whole thing seemed kind of funny. They howled at the part about the triangle, and they were on the floor when I told them about the people who cheered for us in the museum.

Finally I was recovering my long-lost appetite. Our window was open, and the scent of broiling hamburgers wafted in from the coffee shop next door. "I'm starved," I said.

"Maybe we can stick our heads out the window and ask someone to flip us up a burger," Abby offered.

I was dying to go to the coffee shop. I knew Abby had money left. I could repay her at home. And I definitely wouldn't become lost. "Let's sneak out for a snack," I suggested.

Stacey snorted a laugh. "Right."

"I mean it," I insisted.

"Are you nuts?" Abby said. "We're not allowed to leave the room."

"Let alone the hotel," Stacey added.

"The shop is next door," I pressed on. "It's attached. We'll be back in fifteen minutes."

"Claudia, it's almost midnight!" Abby said.

I shrugged. "Which means everyone's asleep, right? What better time than this?"

Stacey looked at Abby. Abby looked at Stacey. They both started giggling.

"You sure you won't get us lost?" Abby asked.

"Very funny," I said.

"Okay," Stacey said, springing to her feet. "But we walk on tiptoes. Melissa may be listening through the walls."

We scurried downstairs, through the lobby, and outside. Trying not to laugh out loud, we ducked into Ralph's Corner Diner.

The food? Greasy. The atmosphere? As charming as a bus station.

But we didn't care.

Forget Le Harborside. Ralph's was the dining experience of the weekend.

"Claudia . . . ?"

I was dreaming about Lynn again. This time, I was holding her snugly in my arms, and Peaches was standing over us, smiling.

"Claudia . . . ?"

The trouble was, Peaches's voice didn't sound like Peaches. It sounded like Melissa.

My eyes fluttered open.

"Claudia? Hi. I'm sorry. Did I wake you?"

Melissa was sitting in the bus seat next to mine.

It was Sunday. When we'd left the Pepperidge Inn that afternoon for our trip home, Melissa had sat with Lily in the back of the bus. Stacey and Abby had taken two seats together. I'd plopped down on the seat behind them.

Yes, we were finally heading for Stoneybrook, after a whirlwind tour of the Philadelphia waterfront and Independence Seaport.

Until that moment, the seat next to mine

had remained empty. (I guess my classmates were still sore at me.) All around me, kids were slumbering away, including Stacey and Abby.

At that moment, I wished I were, too. I was kind of surprised Melissa was talking to me. She'd avoided me all day. Finally she had started sticking with her roommate. (Lily is so sweet. Honestly, I thought she'd blow Melissa off after her rudeness this weekend.)

"Well, yes, I was asleep," I said. "What's up?"

"I'm sorry, Claudia," Melissa said. "I just wanted to . . . you know, *talk*."

"We're talking."

Melissa took a deep breath. "Look, I know you're mad at me. And if you want to yell at me, I wouldn't blame you. Lily did. She said I was being like a puppy dog, running after you and Abby and Stacey, and ignoring her."

"Well . . . " I didn't want to insult Melissa. But Lily was right.

"I didn't mean to be a pest, Claudia. Really. I didn't realize I was. I guess I just liked hanging out with you. You're really funny, and fun to be around."

"It's not that we don't like you, Melissa," I said. "We don't really know you that well —"

"I know, I know. Because I was trying too

hard to be cool. Like you guys." Melissa shrugged and gave me a half smile. "Anyway, I should get back to Lily. I just wanted to come over and say I'm sorry."

"It's okay," I replied. "Apology accepted."

As she walked away, I gazed out the window. We were passing an industrial area of New Jersey. The last time we'd been through here, it had been raining. I'd been thinking about what a terrible godmother I was. What a pest I'd been to Peaches.

A pest.

I thought about Melissa. How she'd almost ruined my weekend. How hearing her voice would make me cringe. How she'd intruded on my time with my friends.

Was *that* the way I'd seemed to Peaches? Nahhh. I was nothing like Melissa. And besides, Peaches and I have been buddies all my life. What had I done to her? I had paid loving visits, bought presents, and given advice.

Every single day.

Many times past dinner.

I tried putting myself in Peaches's shoes. I imagined what it must have felt like to have my niece showing up every day like clockwork. Correcting my mistakes. Doting over my baby. Sticking around after my husband came home. Inviting myself to dinner.

Ugh. What was it Melissa had said to me during our disaster in Philly? "I was only trying to help"?

That sounded familiar.

I sank back into my seat and sighed.

Melissa's apology had made me feel much better.

I owed Peaches. I owed her, big-time.

I must have fallen asleep again, because I was jolted awake when the bus stopped.

Outside my window was the parking lot of Stoneybrook Middle School, dimly lit by streetlamps in the darkness. A small crowd had gathered by the curb. Mom, Dad, and Janine were waving at me, grinning ecstatically.

So were Kristy, Mary Anne, Logan, Mallory, Jessi, and Shannon.

I bopped Abby and Stacey. "Wake up, guys! We're home!"

"Ohhh . . . are we in Hawaii yet?" Abby moaned.

"La-a-a-st stop!" the bus driver called out.

With a *fwoosh*, the door opened.

I rushed out to a sea of familiar faces and happy voices.

"Hi!" Mary Anne shouted. "How was it?"

"Did you bring me home a hoagie?" Kristy asked.

"How were Ben and George and Betsy?" Janine asked.

I hugged and laughed and answered as many questions as I could. Soon I spotted Stacey and Abby straggling out. Just beyond them, the Karps and the Bankses were greeting each other. Everyone looked so happy.

Boy, was it good to be home.

CHAPTER 15

My fingers were shaking as I lifted the receiver of my phone. Carefully I tapped out Peaches's number.

"Hello?"

"Peaches?" I squeaked.

"Claudia? You're back! How was your trip?"

She didn't sound angry. Okay, she didn't exactly sound ready to commandeer the welcome wagon, either, but I had to take what I could get.

I told her about the weekend. I described the sights and the show and the restaurant. (I left out my misadventure with Melissa. That could wait until later.)

"Sounds terrific, Claudia. Well, Lynn missed you very much. She's right here and she's dying to talk to you. Say hi to your godmother, Lynn."

I heard the cutest heavy breathing and gurgling. My heart melted. "Hiiiii!" I cooed. "Oh,

I missed you, too. I hope you behaved. You didn't? Oh, well, that makes two of us."

"Oh?" Peaches said. "Did you leave out any juicy details of your trip?"

I laughed. *Now* Peaches was sounding like her old self. "I'll tell you when I see you in person. Like, maybe tomorrow after school?"

"Well, sure — "

"Only for a short while," I said quickly. "I won't stay more than a half hour or so. Just enough to say hi and chat awhile. I don't want to be in your way."

"Oh. Well, that's very thoughtful of you."

"And I promise I won't be a pest anymore, really —"

"Claudia, you're not a pest," Peaches said. "I'm sorry I yelled at you. I was just stressed out, that's all."

"I know, and I wasn't helping by breathing down your neck every day."

"Look. You are my daughter's godmother. I know how much you love her, and our door will never be closed to you, Claudia. Never."

My throat just choked right up. "Thanks, Peaches," I croaked.

"But you have to give us a little courtesy, that's all. A phone call before you come over, just in case we can't handle a visit at that particular time."

I nodded. "I promise it won't be every day.

I'm so sorry for the way I've been. And I won't butt in with advice so much, or take away your time with Russ, or bring so many gifts —"

"Whoa. Back up. I don't mind the gifts."

I burst into giggles. "Well, in that case, I can't wait to show you the cutest dress I bought in the Gallery . . . "

Peaches was all ears.

I didn't dare tell her I had thought about de-godmotherizing myself. I wiped the idea from my mind.

Forever.

A week later, it became official.

Baby Lynn was christened at the First Congregational Church in Stoneybrook. I, Claudia Lynn Kishi, stood by her side and vowed to take care of her and help her grow up right. I tried not to be weepy, but it didn't work.

Oh, well. Nobody minded when Lynn started crying, so why shouldn't I cry a little, too?

Lynn's godfather was a close friend of Russ's. To cheer me up, he kept whispering jokes.

Some godmother. I alternated between honking my nose into a tissue and fighting back giggles. Then I developed the hiccups.

The worst part was that Kristy taped the

whole thing with her camcorder. And she zoomed in on me a lot.

I guess she was shifting from horror to comedy.

The Godmother, Part One.

Someday Kristy would show it to Lynn, just to embarrass me.

I wouldn't mind a bit. Plenty of good stuff would be on that video, too. The best part was when Peaches handed Lynn to me in the ceremony. Lynn stopped crying right away. She looked at me for a long moment.

And then, in front of the whole gathering, she smiled.

You know what? I don't care what anyone thought.

I knew it wasn't gas.

Dear Reader,

In *Claudia and the World's Cutest Baby*, Claudia is very excited when Peaches and Russ give their baby Claudia's middle name, Lynn. When my parents were expecting me, they picked out two names: John Lawrence and Ann Elizabeth. In the end, I was named Ann Matthews (Matthews is my mother's maiden name). Like Peaches and Russ, my parents were very proud of me. My mother wrote down everything I did in my baby book. For example, my first word was "ba," for bird. Interestingly enough, one of my next words, "ackaminnie," meant ice cream. I'm sure I wasn't the world's cutest baby, but my parents certainly thought I was.

Happy reading,

Ann M Martin

Ann M. Martin

About the Author

ANN MATTHEWS MARTIN was born on August 12, 1955. She grew up in Princeton, NJ, with her parents and her younger sister, Jane.

Although Ann used to be a teacher and then an editor of children's books, she's now a full-time writer. She gets the ideas for her books from many different places. Some are based on personal experiences. Others are based on childhood memories and feelings. Many are written about contemporary problems or events.

All of Ann's characters, even the members of the Baby-sitters Club, are made up. (So is Stoneybrook.) But many of her characters are based on real people. Sometimes Ann names her characters after people she knows, other times she chooses names she likes.

In addition to the Baby-sitters Club books, Ann Martin has written many other books for children. Her favorite is *Ten Kids, No Pets* because she loves big families and she loves animals. Her favorite Baby-sitters Club book is *Kristy's Big Day*. (By the way, Kristy is her favorite baby-sitter!)

Ann M. Martin now lives in New York with her cats, Gussie and Woody. Her hobbies are reading, sewing, and needlework — especially making clothes for children.

Notebook Pages

This Baby-sitters Club book belongs to ______________________.

I am ______________ years old and in the ____________________ grade.

The name of my school is ______________________________________.

I got this BSC book from ______________________________________.

I started reading it on ____________________________________ and finished reading it on ___________________________________.

The place where I read most of this book is ________________.

My favorite part was when _____________________________________.

If I could change anything in the story, it might be the part when ____.

My favorite character in the Baby-sitters Club is ___________.

The BSC member I am most like is ___________________________ because ____.

If I could write a Baby-sitters Club book it would be about ___ ____.

#97 Claudia and the World's Cutest Baby

Claudia thinks her cousin Lynn is the world's cutest baby. The cutest baby I've ever seen is ______________________________.

Russ and Peaches choose Lynn as the baby's name because it is Claudia's middle name. My two favorite names for a baby girl are ______________________________ and ______________________________. My two favorite names for a baby boy are ______________________________ and ______________________________. Claudia's cousin Lynn is a very sweet baby. When I was a baby, I was very ______________________________. The first word I ever said was ______________________________. The second word I ever said was ______________________________. If I had been born a boy instead of a girl (or a girl instead of a boy), I would have been named ______________________________. If I could pick any name for myself right now, it would be ______________________________.

CLAUDIA'S

Finger painting at 3...

A spooky sitting adventur

Sitting for two of my favorite charges --
Jamie and Lucy Newton.

SCRAPBOOK

...oil painting at 13!

my family. Mom and Dad, me and Janine... and we'll never forget Mimi.

Interior art by Angelo Tillery

Read all the books
about **Claudia**
in the Baby-sitters Club series
by Ann M. Martin

\# 2 *Claudia and the Phantom Phone Calls*
Someone mysterious is calling Claudia!

\# 7 *Claudia and Mean Janine*
Claudia's big sister is super smart . . . and super mean.

#12 *Claudia and the New Girl*
Claudia might give up the club — and it's all Ashley's fault.

#19 *Claudia and the Bad Joke*
When Claudia baby-sits for a practical joker, she's headed for big trouble.

#26 *Claudia and the Sad Good-bye*
Claudia never thought anything bad would happen to her grandmother, Mimi.

#33 *Claudia and the Great Search*
Claudia thinks she was adopted — and no one told her about it.

#40 *Claudia and the Middle School Mystery*
How could anyone accuse *Claudia* of cheating?

#49 *Claudia and the Genius of Elm Street*
Baby-sitting for a seven-year-old genius makes Claudia feel like a world-class dunce.

#56 *Keep Out, Claudia!*
Who wouldn't want Claudia for a baby-sitter?

#63 *Claudia's ~~Freind~~ Friend*
Claudia and Shea can't spell — but they can be friends!

#71 *Claudia and the Perfect Boy*
Love is in the air when Claudia starts a personals column in the school paper.

#78 *Claudia and Crazy Peaches*
Claudia's crazy Aunt Peaches is back in town. Let the games begin!

#85 *Claudia Kishi, Live from WSTO!*
Claudia wins a contest to have her own radio show.

#91 *Claudia and the First Thanksgiving*
Claudia's in the middle of a big Thanksgiving controversy!

#97 *Claudia and the World's Cutest Baby*
Claudia can't take her eyes off of her adorable new niece.

Mysteries:

6 *The Mystery at Claudia's House*
Claudia's room has been ransacked! Can the baby-sitters track down whodunnit?

#11 *Claudia and the Mystery at the Museum*
Burglaries, forgeries . . . something crooked is going on at the new museum in Stoneybrook!

#16 *Claudia and the Clue in the Photograph*
Has Claudia caught a thief — on film?

#21 *Claudia and the Recipe for Danger*
There's nothing half-baked about the attempts to sabotage a big cooking contest!

Portrait Collection:

Claudia's Book
Claudia's design for living.

Look for #98

DAWN AND TOO MANY SITTERS

As Claud passed around the snacks, Kristy called out, "Listen up, please! Here are the rules for Baby-sitters in Training."

"Give me those!" Jeff whispered, grabbing the pretzels from Jordan.

Kristy harrumphed. "We'll start by taking you on jobs, one boy per sitter."

"What about Little League days?" Byron asked.

"Work around them," Kristy answered. "A commitment is a commitment — "

"Sto-o-o-op!" Adam yelled as three arms reached into the Famous Amos box on his lap.

"Your job is to listen to whatever your sitter says," Kristy forged on. "In some cases you may be one-on-one with — "

"*Brrrrrup!*" burped Adam. Then, "Excuse me," he squeaked. His face turned bright red. Jeff, Byron, and Jordan were trying so hard not to laugh that their shoulders were shaking.

"Ahem," Kristy said. "As I was saying, you will work your hardest, and you will be paid. Your sitter will give you one quarter of her earnings — "

"A quarter?" Jordan looked dismayed.

Next to him, Byron suddenly started squirming. He shot Jeff a nervous glance.

"Twenty-five percent," Kristy clarified. "Now, you'll keep in mind that we're doing this for you. Despite the fact that we desperately need to save money for our Hawaii trip — "

Now Adam was whispering something to my brother. Jeff's eyes grew wide and he clapped his hand over his face.

That was when I noticed the odor. It seeped up from the floor, spreading like an unexpected warm front.

"And most of all, be polite, be cheerful, and give one hundred and ten percent," Kristy droned on. "What do you say, guys?"

Jordan crinkled up his nose. "Who farted?"

Well, forget it. Those boys were rolling on the floor. Convulsing with laughter. Screaming.

The Baby-sitters Club titles continued...

❑ MG48222-X	#78	Claudia and the Crazy Peaches	$3.50
❑ MG48223-8	#79	Mary Anne Breaks the Rules	$3.50
❑ MG48224-6	#80	Mallory Pike, #1 Fan	$3.50
❑ MG48225-4	#81	Kristy and Mr. Mom	$3.50
❑ MG48226-2	#82	Jessi and the Troublemaker	$3.50
❑ MG48235-1	#83	Stacey vs. the BSC	$3.50
❑ MG48228-9	#84	Dawn and the School Spirit War	$3.50
❑ MG48236-X	#85	Claudi Kishli, Live from WSTO	$3.50
❑ MG48227-0	#86	Mary Anne and Camp BSC	$3.50
❑ MG48237-8	#87	Stacey and the Bad Girls	$3.50
❑ MG22872-2	#88	Farewell, Dawn	$3.50
❑ MG22873-0	#89	Kristy and the Dirty Diapers	$3.50
❑ MG22874-9	#90	Welcome to the BSC, Abby	$3.50
❑ MG22875-1	#91	Claudia and the First Thanksgiving	$3.50
❑ MG22876-5	#92	Mallory's Christmas Wish	$3.50
❑ MG22877-3	#93	Mary Anne and the Memory Garden	$3.99
❑ MG22878-1	#94	Stacey McGill, Super Sitter	$3.99
❑ MG45575-3		Logan's Story Special Edition Readers' Request	$3.25
❑ MG47118-X		Logan Bruno, Boy Baby-sitter Special Edition Readers' Request	$3.50
❑ MG47756-0		Shannon's Story Special Edition	$3.50
❑ MG47686-6		The Baby-sitters Club Guide to Baby-sitting	$3.25
❑ MG47314-X		The Baby-sitters Club Trivia and Puzzle Fun Book	$2.50
❑ MG48400-1		BSC Portrait Collection: Claudia's Book	$3.50
❑ MG22864-1		BSC Portrait Collection: Dawn's Book	$3.50
❑ MG48399-4		BSC Portrait Collection: Stacey's Book	$3.50
❑ MG47151-1		The Baby-sitters Club Chain Letter	$14.95
❑ MG48295-5		The Baby-sitters Club Secret Santa	$14.95
❑ MG45074-3		The Baby-sitters Club Notebook	$2.50
❑ MG44783-1		The Baby-sitters Club Postcard Book	$4.95

Available wherever you buy books...or use this order form.

Scholastic Inc., P.O. Box 7502, 2931 E. McCarty Street, Jefferson City, MO 65102

Please send me the books I have checked above. I am enclosing $________
(please add $2.00 to cover shipping and handling). Send check or money order–no cash or C.O.D.s please.

Name ______________________________ Birthdate________________

Address ____

City________________________ State/Zip ________________

Please allow four to six weeks for delivery. Offer good in the U.S. only. Sorry, mail orders are not available to residents of Canada. Prices subject to change.

BSC795

More titles ➡